Hobo Pete and the Ghost Train

Book I

By Sandy Pheat

Freebird Publishers

www.FreebirdPublishers.com

Freebird Publishers

Box 541, North Dighton, MA 02764

Info@FreebirdPublishers.com

www.FreebirdPublishers.com

All Freebird Publishers titles, imprints and distributed
lines are available at special quantity discounts for
bulk purchases for sales promotions, premiums, fund-
raising, educational or institutional use.

ISBN: 978-0-9913591-0-3

Library of Congress Control Number: 2014947284

Printed in the United States of America

DEDICATION

This book is dedicated to all the children of the world who have suffered but endured, including my own sons. May you all grow to be strong, courageous, and compassionate to others who struggle. –Sandy

AKNOWLEDGEMENTS

Many thanks to Diane and all of the staff of Freebird Publishers for their hard work, guidance and patience, without which this book would not have been possible.

Special thanks to Thomas and Pat Atkinson, Corina Holmes, Laiza Chavez and Jose Porras-Muniz for their support and encouragement.

Hobo - /hō bō/ n. (pl. -OES or -OS)

A wandering worker; a tramp [19th C., orig. unknown.]

— Oxford American Dictionary

The technical description of a Hobo should not and cannot accurately describe what a true Hobo is or was. A wandering worker? Yes. A tramp? Yes. But there is so much more to know about Hobos.

The following is a story of one such Hobo, and of how mistaken people can be when they judge someone without knowing their past, and just how courageous and brave the downtrodden can be when called upon.

INTRODUCTION

The Hobo Pete and the Ghost Train series of books offers an inspirational line of stories for young and older readers worldwide. The books share stories of danger and excitement as well as opening a spirit-world dimension. The initial book in the series begins in Carbon Hollow, a small town where miracles of sorts begin to happen as the Ghost Train signals impending doom for those who hear it.

As the story unfolds its characters are both frightened and victimized by the evil conductor who has the mission of collecting the dead. The battle that Hobo Pete and Ben begin in the first book continues with ever-increasing intensity and mysterious aspects while children and adults alike are drawn into this journey.

There are not many people on the planet that are not directly affected by the mere existence of a train. There are many opportunities to join in on the journey of the Ghost Train. E-mail Hobo Pete at Sandy@SandyPheat.com and join in on the fun!

All Aboooooaaaaaard!

Illustration 1: The Ghost Train

CHAPTER 1

Carbon Hollow, West Virginia is one fine place to be in the spring time. Cool in the morning and warm in the afternoon.

A small, quiet, friendly town, just the way I like it. Although, it hasn't always been so quiet and friendly. No sir, we've had our share of excitement. But that was a long time ago.

I've lived here most of my sixty-two years save for the four years I spent in the Army, which included two tours of duty in that living hell in Southeast Asia back in '68.

Vietnam! My God, just the thought of the name brings back a flood of horrible memories. Fighting off the Viet Cong, the smell of napalm and burnt bodies. But I made it out alive, which is more than I can say for some of my friends, God rest their souls.

I had just finished mowing the grass and was sitting on the front porch swing, swaying back and forth, sipping on a cool glass of iced tea, admiring the color of spring in the trees and newly planted flower gardens of our neighbors, when I saw the dark blue SUV with a U-Haul trailer in tow, turn the corner and head in our direction.

I stood, walked to the front door and shouted inside,

"Honey, they're here."

From somewhere in the house my wife answered, "I'll be right there."

Standing at the top of the front porch steps I watched as our one and only daughter, Katie, pulled the SUV into the drive.

She had no sooner stopped the truck when the passenger door flew open and out popped my grandson, Dustin, who was running and stumbling up the sidewalk and steps. His blonde hair was a mess and I couldn't help but notice that, for an eight year old, he certainly was tall.

He shouted, "Grandpa!" as I bent down and held my arms wide. He almost knocked me over as he wrapped his arms around my neck. I said, "Peanut, boy am I happy to see you." Dustin was grinning from ear to ear at the use of the nickname I'd given him.

I lifted him and the pain ripped through my lower back and legs. After all these years the shrapnel still gave me fits. I did the best I could not to show the pain. It was important that I be strong for them – especially now.

Katie had married a soldier and he was in the desert in Iraq fighting his war. Ours was Vietnam, and I wondered what war Dustin would be in. It just seemed like we were always at war with someone. Kevin, Katie and Dustin had moved around from one military base to another for years, but we finally convinced her to bring Dustin and stay with us for a while, at least until Kevin returned from the war. We'd discussed it and decided it would be best for them to be near family. After all, being alone, waiting for news that your husband is coming home, or not, can be so hard.

I said to Dustin, "Guess what, I've got a surprise for you."

"Really, Grandpa, what is it?" he said, eyes wide and half shouting.

Katie was at the bottom of the front steps trying to manage three suitcases at once. She said, "Hey, Sarge, since you're obviously well enough to be lifting that little rascal, do you think I could get some help here?"

I looked down at her, smiled and said, "Of course, honey, I was just sayin' hello to my favorite grandson."

Dustin said, "I thought I was your *only* grandson."

"You are, Peanut. You're also my favorite."

Mama came through the screen door and took Dustin from me, "Take it easy honey, before you hurt him."

Katie said, "Put him down Momma, he's too big to be picked up like that."

When she put Dustin down he ran down the steps with me and said, "I'll help you, Grandpa, so we can hurry up and see my surprise."

Katie rolled her eyes, "Okay, okay, you two go ahead. Me and Mom will unload the trailer."

I was about to protest but Dustin was tugging on my hand. "Well, all right, but we won't be long and I'll be back to help."

Again Katie rolled her eyes and smiled. "Sure you will, Sarge. Now get."

I led Dustin to the garage and once inside I opened a cabinet door and pulled out a brand spanking new Zebco 303 fishing rod and reel. Dustin's eyes bulged, "Wow, is that my surprise, Grandpa?"

He snatched it from my hands before I could answer. "Hey, take it easy, Peanut, that rod already has a hook on it."

"Can we go fishing, Grandpa, can we?"

"Well, I don't see why not. But first we have to help the womenfolk unload the trailer. Remember, we promised … we'll go after that."

Dustin was anxious, "Do you think we'll catch something Grandpa?"

"Well, I just happen to know of a secret fishing-hole where there's so many fish you might catch five with one hook."

He wasn't sure if I was telling the truth or just playing. "Can we go now and help with the trailer when we get back?"

I laughed and shook my head, "Not unless you want to sleep in the doghouse."

Dustin's left eye went up as he said, "I didn't know you had a dog Grandpa."

"Well, that's just an expression. It means we'd be in trouble if we didn't help the womenfolk and tried to go fishing first."

Dustin was still confused, "So, you *don't* have a dog?"

I reached down, tousled his hair, and said, "No, Peanut, I don't have a dog. Listen, why don't you put your new rod and reel on the table over there, for now. The sooner we unload the trailer, the sooner we can go fishing."

Dustin headed for my old work bench as I went to open the garage door. From behind me I heard him say, "Grandpa, what's all this?"

I turned to see Dustin standing over the old army footlocker I had placed under my work bench. He held the lid up and was looking inside.

Before I could reach him, he'd already pulled an old photo album out and was thumbing through it.

He'd stopped at a page that had a torn and faded newspaper article. He was trying to read it when I slowly took it from his hand.

I said, "Peanut, there ain't nothing of interest in that old album. Why don't we go unload the trailer?"

"Grandpa, I saw your name in that article."

I was frozen in place. It had been a long time since I'd seen the photo album or the article. Oh, why hadn't I thrown that old locker full of junk away years ago?

As I held the photo album in my hand, Dustin tugged on my shirt and said, "Are you okay, Grandpa?"

I realized that my mind had drifted and for a moment I was back in time, all the way to 1963.

Dustin asked, "Who is Hobo Pete?"

I said, "What's that, Peanut?"

He pointed to the article in my hand and said, "Who is

Hobo Pete?"

I closed the lid on the locker and sat down, motioning for Dustin to sit beside me. I started thumbing through the pages of the album until I found the photo I was looking for. It was a black and white picture of three young boys clad only in blue jeans with their arms around each other's shoulders.

I showed Dustin the photo and said, "That's my brother Matt there on the right and our best friend Ben on the left. This photo was taken in 1963, not long after that article was written."

Dustin asked, "Did you know Hobo Pete, Grandpa?"

I raised my head and stared out the open garage door, seeing all the way back to 1963. "Yes, I knew Hobo Pete; he was our friend, but only for a short time."

"Tell me about him Grandpa, tell me."

I nodded and searched my memory from fifty years earlier, and started to tell Dustin the story of Hobo Pete.

"Well, Peanut, we were inseparable. Where you saw one, you saw the other two. Matt and Ben were ten years old and I was twelve. Me being two years older I guess you could say I was the leader of our little trio…"

Illustration 2: Ben, Matt and Andy

CHAPTER 2

We were standing on the corner just outside of the Carbon Hollow Middle School waiting for our parents to pick us up.

As usual it was me, my younger brother Matt and our best friend Ben. They'd just walked over from the elementary school two blocks away and were being their typical selves, asking a bunch of questions.

"Listen, fellas, I've got important stuff goin' on, so why don't y'all just walk home."

Ben said, "Why would we walk when your parents will be here soon to give us a ride?"

Matt chimed in, "Yeah, Andy, why would we do somethin' stupid like that?"

I just shook my head; these guys were going to mess everything up, and it looked as though there was no getting rid of them.

"Well okay, but I need you guys to be quiet while I think. I've got grown up things goin' on, and I need to concentrate."

"But you ain't grown up, you're only two years older than us." Ben complained.

"Boys, you just don't understand, once you move up to

middle school, you have to start acting like grown-ups and let go of kids' games."

Matt asked, "Can you show us some grown-up stuff?"

At that moment I caught sight of them heading in our direction.

Maryanne Taylor and Andrea Fisher, just like two crossed fingers they were always together – kinda like us boys.

"Okay, you want to see some grown-up stuff, get yourselves behind the tree and observe."

As Matt and Ben ducked behind the big old oak tree that stood tall and wide on the corner of the school grounds Ben said, "Whacha gonna do, Andy?"

"I'm gonna give you guys a lesson in courtin' womenfolk." I said as I struck a pose with one hand resting on the oak tree and the other hand on my hip. I envisioned myself as James Dean, or maybe Elvis Presley.

Matt and Ben were snickering behind the tree and I whispered under my breath, "Quiet, you idiots."

I stood there trying to look cool and disinterested. As Maryanne and Andrea passed, they stared at me and when I knew I had Maryanne's full attention, I raised my left eyebrow.

The girls busted into laughter and scurried along as Matt and Ben stepped out from behind the tree, with incredulous looks on their faces.

Matt said, "That's it?"

"That's it, boys." I replied feeling good about how well my plan had gone.

Ben was on the verge of laughing himself when he said, "But you didn't say anything."

"Yeah," Matt joined in, "you just did that stupid thing with your eye."

"Awe, don't you boys know nothin'? I was speaking to her with my eyes. You two wouldn't understand 'cause you ain't grown-up yet."

Ben giggled and said, "What was you sayin', Andy, I

mean, with your eyes?"

"Well, I was lettin' her know I was interested and if she was of a mind to, I'd be her boyfriend."

"Oh, I get it," Ben replied, "kinda like, body talk."

"That's right, now you're getting it."

Ben said, "And when they laughed and ran away, what was they tryin' to say?"

Matt burst out laughing, "I think they was tellin' Andy to stay away from them or else they was gonna call the sheriff."

Ben was laughing also, and said, "Yeah, and maybe Andy could make that eye thing again to tell the sheriff not to take him to the looney bin."

"Okay, that's it, now you've done it!" I grabbed Ben and put him into a headlock.

Matt jumped on me from behind and we hit the ground in a tangled mess. We were really kicking up some dust when we heard the horn blow.

We stopped wrestling and looked up to see Mom's new Pontiac sitting at the curb and our parents staring at us from inside the car, obviously not pleased with our horseplay.

Matt and Ben pushed me to the ground as they ran to the car, both wanting to get a window seat.

I climbed into the backseat, forced to sit between them.

Mom turned and checked us out from head to toe. Without saying a word we knew she didn't approve of our wrestling.

When she turned to face forward I nudged Matt and Ben and half-whispered, "You see, without saying a word." I pointed towards Mom and pulled a finger across my throat. They nodded their understanding. A block later we passed Maryanne and Andrea as they were walking down the sidewalk. Ben lunged over me, and together with Matt, they hung their heads out the window and began moving their eyebrows up and down to mock me.

I punched them in the ribs and when they screamed

Mom spun around and gave us another look. That was strike two, we decided not to go for strike three and settled down. When dad reached the corner and was about to turn I chanced one last look out the rear window. Just then Maryanne raised a hand and gave me a little wave and a smile. I turned back around and thought to myself, I knew it, she likes me.

Illustration 3: Andrea and Maryanne

CHAPTER 3

As soon as we walked into the house Mom said, "Homework first, boys."

We were anxious to watch our favorite shows, *Andy Griffith*, *My Three Sons* and *McHale's Navy* but we knew no amount of pleading would change Mom's command. So we headed to our room, and set about doing our homework. Since moving to middle school the class work and homework had gotten tougher, but I managed.

It took us an hour to finish the homework and we were able to catch an episode of *McHale's Navy* before the boring stuff came on – the news; we hated it, but Dad seemed to enjoy it.

I said to Matt and Ben, "There's still a couple of hours of sunlight left, what do you say we head out to the treehouse and put the finishing touches on the door?"

They agreed and after I grabbed Dad's tool box from the garage, we jumped on our bikes and were about to head down the driveway, when Mom shouted through the screen of the back door, "Y'all be back before sunset or you'll have to eat your supper cold."

"Okay, Mom, we will." I said.

We'd been building us a treehouse for a month now

and it was finally finished. The only thing left was hanging the door.

We'd built our treehouse in a thick patch of forest about a mile from our house, just on the edge of Mr. Brown's farm.

As we stood at the trunk of the old oak tree and looked up at our treehouse, a sense of pride came over us. We'd done a good job, but to give credit where credit is due, we couldn't have built it without Dad's and Mr. Brown's help.

Carbon Hollow didn't have a lot for young boys to do and they knew a treehouse would give us boys a place to go and let our imaginations run wild, not to mention the awe and respect we'd get from the other boys in town.

After all, a treehouse puts you in elite status compared to, say, a trampoline. Of course, Johnny Graham had a swimming pool in his back yard, and there's no way to top that. Although a treehouse should be considered a close second.

The day before, we had cut the wood and nailed together a door. The only thing left to do was to hoist it up to the treehouse and nail the hinges in place.

I was the strongest so I would be the one who hoisted the door. I climbed the ladder, which was just a bunch of pieces of wood planks nailed to the tree, until I was sitting on my knees inside the treehouse. After looping the rope through a pulley Dad had secured to a limb, I lowered it to the ground.

Matt tied the end of the rope to the door, and with Ben's help they lifted it as high as they could. I said, "I hope you tied that rope tight, I'd hate for it to come loose and hit you on the head, and I'd end up with a ree-tard for a brother."

Matt said, "You just be careful and don't drop it on purpose, 'cause I'd sure hate to be a ree-tard."

Ben was grunting and red in the face, "Will you two quit your yappin', this door's gettin' heavy!"

I tugged and pulled until the door was inside.

Matt and Ben climbed the ladder and together we finally got it in place and nailed down good and secure.

It was a little lopsided but it was good enough; we sat back and enjoyed a Goo-Goo Cluster as we admired our work.

We'd built us a good treehouse, and we would spend many a day in it over the coming months, daydreaming, joking and just being the boys we were.

I said, "It's gettin' late guys, we better get going. Besides, I'm hungry."

Matt asked, "What's Mom cooking tonight?"

"Come on, Matt, it's Wednesday, you know Mom always cooks meatloaf on Wednesdays."

"I know Mom always cooks meatloaf on Wednesdays, I just forgot what day it was is all." Matt explained.

Ben chimed in, trying to support Matt, "I forgot what day it was too, Andy."

I rolled my eyes, "Does it really matter, Ben? You're going to eat with us no matter what Mom's cooking, right?"

"Of course I am. Your Mom has the best food in town, I just wanted to get my taste buds ready."

"And how would you know she has the best food in town, you been eating at every house in town?"

Before Ben could respond I climbed down the ladder. We were just getting on our bikes when we heard something rustling a little deeper into the brush.

We tried to see if there was movement coming from the direction of the rustling sound but didn't see anything.

Then we heard it again, only this time it seemed closer and I was sure I heard a grunting sound. Suddenly, I realized it was almost dark and for some reason, I was scared.

It could be anything; a bobcat, a black bear or maybe even *somebody*. We were frozen in place, listening to the sound as it grew closer and closer.

Finally, I shouted, "Let's move guys, fast!" Never had I

been so scared and we peddled our bikes faster than ever before.

There was no looking back. Only fast peddling, and I don't think a one of us took a breath until we'd turned down our street and could see our house.

As we pulled our bikes into the garage I noticed that Ben was having trouble breathing and was holding his chest.

Ben had a weak heart and we never talked about it much, but the fact was if he didn't get a heart donor soon, the doctor said we should prepare for the worst.

I put my hand on Ben's shoulder, "Try to relax Ben, relax and breathe slowly."

Matt locked eyes with me and I could see the fear, we both knew what the other was thinking.

Ben finally got his breathing under control and he said, "Awe come on guys, don't look so gloomy, I ain't dead yet."

I wrapped my arm around Ben's shoulder and said, "Don't say that Ben, you're gonna be around for a long time, I'm sure of it."

Ben was a tough nut, I'll give him that. He pushed me away, "Don't go gettin' all mushy on me. Besides, you two don't look any better, y'all looked like you just pooped your pants.

We all laughed a little harder than was called for. Mostly, I think, because we didn't want to think about Ben's heart condition. "You might be right Ben, I do smell something."

Ben and I looked toward Matt and he said, "It was just a fart."

I laughed and Ben said, "Are you sure it was just a fart? Are you sure there ain't no lumps in that fart?"

Matt balled up a fist and reared back at Ben, "You'll be the one with the lumpy farts when I get through with you."

As he lunged for Ben I stepped between them, "Okay,

that's enough, let's go eat."

Ben stuck his tongue out at Matt and Matt shook his fist at Ben as I pushed them towards the back door of our house.

The smell of Mom's cooking hit us, reminding us just how hungry we were.

Before stepping into the house Matt tugged on my shirt stopping me and said, "Andy, what do you think it was?"

Ben and Matt were staring at me, waiting for an answer. After all, I was older and supposed to have all the answers.

"I don't know guys, probably just an old possum or something. We'll go track it tomorrow."

They weren't so sure it was a possum, and to tell the truth, neither was I.

I tried to comfort them, "Listen you two, if we're goin' to have a treehouse in the woods, we're gonna have to scare 'em off, that's all."

This seemed to ease their minds and I said, "Now let's eat."

CHAPTER 4

Hobo Pete watched the boys as they disappeared down the trail. He'd scared them pretty good, and he laughed and mumbled, "I bet they don't slow down 'til they're home."

He stood at the base of the oak tree and looked up at the treehouse. Not bad he thought, but maybe he should give it a little closer look. Maybe those boys left some food behind, and he sure could use something to eat.

After managing the step ladder nailed up the side of the tree he sat inside trying to catch his breath. The climb was a good twenty feet and he wasn't a spring chicken anymore.

He looked around hoping to find something to eat but found nothing, not even a candy wrapper. Hobo Pete sat on the floor with his legs hanging out the door. The sun was sitting over the hilltops and the view of the shadows climbing over the trees was spectacular. He'd always been an outdoorsman, and had an appreciation for the beautiful landscape and the sounds the night brought with it. After a while he laid back and closed his eyes. His thoughts were on the boys, they were maybe ten or twelve years old, the same age as his children had they lived.

A tear formed at the corner of his eye and ran down his dark and dirty cheek, leaving a clean streak that looked like a scar. It felt good here in the treehouse, the air seemed cleaner and it was dry, unlike the cold, dark and damp cave he lived in. Maybe he'd just sleep here tonight, he thought. Maybe he'd scare the boys enough so they wouldn't come back. Then he'd have the treehouse all to himself. No, that wouldn't be right, those boys needed a place like this. A place to get away and be themselves, to be boys. They would share secrets here, they would let their imaginations run wild.

They would be soldiers fighting off the enemy, or maybe big game hunters sitting around bragging about who nailed the biggest catch. They would discuss football, baseball and girls. And they would share a friendship that would last a lifetime. No, he decided, he would not scare them away. This was *their* treehouse, and they'd worked hard to build it. A lot of dreaming would be done here and that was a good thing, boys should have dreams. As long as the dreams weren't horrible ones like he himself had. Of course he wasn't a boy anymore. He was a man, a man who'd seen too much death and tragedy to ever have a peaceful night's sleep again. Lord what he'd give to have just one night without the nightmares, just one.

Before he knew it, he drifted off to sleep, but it was short-lived; around midnight he was snatched awake by that awful sound, the screeching, screaming sound that had awakened him so many times before.

And like always, he was unable to move, almost as if he was being held down and forced to listen. He moaned, "Nooo, God, not again!"

He could hear the rumbling sound of the train's engines, thundering almost. And the train's whistle was not so much a whistle, as it was a screaming sound.

That was it he thought, screaming, hundreds of people screaming all at once. One-hundred and seventy-seven people to be exact – he knew the number well. It was deafening and grew louder and louder until all at once the sound was gone.

Just like that Pete heard only the crickets and critters of the night. No train, no screaming, and the pressure inside his head was gone too, allowing him to move around. "Why, God?" he said to himself, "Why did they have to die?"

He rolled on his side and sobbed, the tears pouring from his eyes and splattering the wooden floor of the treehouse. Before Pete was able to pull himself from the floor and make his way down the ladder, he had one last thought; "Who was it this time?"

CHAPTER 5

It was almost eight o'clock by the time we finished eating supper. We were hanging out on the back porch steps, our bellies full, enjoying the night. Mom called out from the kitchen, "Ben, your Momma just called and said you gotta get home now, or else she was gonna lock you out."

Ben rolled his eyes, "I better go guys, see you tomorrow."

"Want me to come with you?"

This upset Ben, he didn't like being pampered like some baby. "I know my way home, Andy! Besides who would help *you* get back home?"

We watched Ben disappear down our street just as Mom said, "You boys get on in here and get your baths, it'll be bedtime soon."

"Awe Mom, can't we hang out a little longer?" Matt asked.

"Now!" she replied with a sharp tone, and that was it. We didn't dare test the wrath of Mom.

To my recollection Mom had never laid a hand on me or Matt, but something told us not to press her. There was just something in the way she looked at you and the tone of her voice which warned that just under the surface of her sweet demeanor was something that would bust out and take us boys to a place we didn't want to go.

No, we never pressed. Better to do as we were told and live to be an adult, so we headed to our rooms.

Later on, while laying in bed after bathing and putting our pajamas on, Matt asked, "Andy, do you think that noise we heard was that old hobo?"

I thought for a moment, "Maybe, he's got to live somewhere; maybe he stays in the woods at night."

"What are we gonna do if it was him? You know he's killed a hundred kids like us."

"Come on Matt, you know that's just stories the town folk made up because they don't know him."

"How do you know the stories ain't true?" Andy

"Cause, if the stories were true, Sheriff Bryson would have done locked him up by now. Besides, he ain't killed us yet and we've been going out there a lot lately."

Matt said, "Not yet."

"Shut up and go to sleep." I rolled over and closed my eyes.

It seemed like I'd just fallen asleep, but it was actually around midnight when I heard it. I shot straight up on my bed and looked over at Matt who was wide awake and had a frightened look on his face. From outside the open window the noise got louder and louder; a rumbling sound and screaming like we'd heard before. It had been awhile since we'd heard it last, but there it was again, and just like before it was gone as quickly as it had come. Matt was shaking and I thought my heart would bust out of my chest.

Matt asked, "Who do you think it was this time?"

I just shook my head, too afraid to speak. I climbed out of bed, shut the window and joined Matt in his bed. We laid there staring at the ceiling and it was a long time before we drifted off to sleep again.

We'd heard the train before as I said, and every time we

heard it, someone would die. The last time it was a drunk driver up on Highway 84. He lost control of his pick-up truck and drove off a bluff.

It was frightening for us boys, and for the life of us we couldn't understand why no one else heard the Ghost Train ... that's the name we'd given it.

After all, it had to be a ghost train, because there were no railroad tracks running through Carbon Hollow.

Ben always heard the train too, and tomorrow we'd learn who died.

Illustration 4: The Boys' Treehouse

CHAPTER 6

The following morning Matt and I hardly said a word during breakfast, and on the ride to Ben's house to pick him up for school, we sat silent in the backseat.

Mom looked over her shoulder at us and said, "You boys sure are quiet this morning, what's going on?"

We hadn't told a soul about the Ghost Train, and we weren't going to, either. People would start thinking we were crazy; and crazy kids don't have friends.

Mom was suspicious and waiting for an answer, I had to think of something quick so I said, "We're sick Mom. I think it was all those Goo-Goo Clusters we ate yesterday."

Mom frowned, "Well that's it then, and from now on you boys are restricted from eating candy."

Dad smiled and asked Mom, "Are you restricting them forever. That seems kinda harsh."

After a moment Mom amended her directive, "Okay, no more candy before supper."

We agreed to her instructions, happy to have the discussion about something other than what was really on our minds.

As we pulled up to the school and got out, Mom said, "If you boys get to feeling worse, y'all be sure to go by the nurse's station. You should have told me you were sick before we left the house, I could have given you some Castor Oil."

Matt, Ben and I had the same thought at the same time. We'd rather die a slow death than to take any more Castor Oil; we'd tried it before and it was worse than any belly ache we'd ever had.

"Don't worry Mom, we're feeling better already."

We watched them drive away, and Ben asked, "Did y'all hear it?"

Matt and I nodded our heads and I said, "We'll meet after school and talk about it. You know it's not good to say anything around here, in case somebody's listening. Now y'all get on to school."

Matt and Ben turned and headed for the elementary school. I watched them for the longest time, lost in thought. I wondered again why we were the only ones who heard the train, and who had died this time?

As I walked towards my first period class with my head hanging down and my mind drifting, I didn't even notice Maryanne and Andrea until I had already passed them.

A small quiet voice said, "Hi Andy, ain't you gonna say good mornin'?"

When I looked up I was staring into her blue eyes and I was almost speechless. Finally I spoke, "Oh hi, I'm sorry, I guess my mind was somewhere else."

They were giggling at the way they'd caught me off-guard. Here I was supposed to be cool and calm, instead I was shaking like a leaf, funny how girls have that effect on a boy.

Maryanne said, "You know my Daddy owns Taylor's Grocery, right?"

I was confused, what a strange statement, all I could think of was, "Uh, yeah."

Maryanne smiled and all I could do was stare. She said, "Well, Daddy's looking for someone to stock shelves this summer. You know, a stock boy?"

Between her blue eyes and perfect smile, she had me dizzy. Come on boy, I thought, get yourself together. She's trying to tell you something, what was it? Oh yeah, her Dad owns a store, something about the stock market and shelves.

I mumbled, "That's great."

She and Andrea giggled and walked away, and I realized what a knucklehead I must have looked like.

I slapped my forehead and thought, *Stupid!*

As I continued on to class it finally hit me exactly what Maryanne was trying to tell me. She was saying to get a job at her Dad's store. And why? So she could see more of me, that's why. *Stupid!*

Mrs. Collins' first period class was one of my favorites. She taught history, and for some reason that subject had always fascinated me.

Once we were settled into our seats, Mrs. Collins said, "Boys and girls, I have an announcement to make; as you will notice, Toby Reed is not in class today. He had a passing in his family."

So there it was, one of Toby's family had died. All the others had been someone like the drunk driver out on the highway, who I didn't know at all.

This was different though, I'd met most of Toby's family ... this one was close to home.

Mrs. Collins continued, "I want everyone to bow their heads in a moment of silence and prayer for Toby's grandmother, Mrs. Emma Reed, who passed away last night after losing her fight with cancer."

I lowered my head like everyone else, but instead of praying my mind was racing with thoughts of the Ghost Train.

Why? That was the burning question I couldn't figure out. Why were we the only ones who heard the train? Why didn't someone else hear it? Or was there someone else, and they were afraid to talk about it too? Before I opened my eyes I thought about Toby. Besides Matt and Ben, he was probably my next closest friend. I felt bad for his family. When people die I always feel bad, so I'd come up with a way to deal with my sorrow. I'd try to remember something good about that person, and would burn that memory into my brain. So I now thought about the time I was invited to a cookout at Toby's house. The Reed family had some relatives in from out of town and Toby's grandmother had made some biscuits that were so good they were more like cake than biscuits. From that day forward I would always have happy memories of Toby's grandmother and her biscuits.

CHAPTER 7

Sheriff Bryson was sitting behind his desk, finishing the last of the day's paperwork when he heard the commotion.

People were talking loudly just outside his office and when he got up to open the door they crowded in, pushing him backwards into his desk. He recognized them, there were maybe fifteen in all, most of them women. They were pointing their fingers at him and all trying to speak at once.

The sheriff let out a loud whistle and this quieted the crowd somewhat. He said, "What in heaven's name is goin' on with you folks?" Again they all spoke at once, and again he let out a loud whistle. "Come on, folks, you all are gonna have to calm down and tell me what happened, one at a time." He caught the eye of Mrs. Barker, who seemed to be the leader of the pack, "Nell, why don't you just tell me what the problem is."

The others opened their mouths to speak but the sheriff held his hand up, stopping them.

Nell Barker, the oldest living school teacher in Carbon Hollow said, "You must do something, we demand it!"

Sheriff Bryson smiled, "And just what is it you dem… uh, want me to do, Nell?"

"It's that old hobo living out in the woods, he's gone

too far this time," replied the teacher.

The sheriff rolled his eyes at the mention of the hobo. He'd heard it a hundred times before and at least once a month a vigilante party of town folks would get in a tizzy over the fact that Carbon Hollow had a stranger living out in the woods.

"Nell, what is it you allege he's done this time?"

The sarcasm was not lost on the teacher and she gave him a harsh look. A look he'd seen many times in his younger years as a student in Mrs. Barker's third period class.

"I'll tell you what he's done! I caught him peeking in my bedroom window last night, just as I was preparing for bed. And that's no allegation, that's the truth!"

Murmurs from some of the other women only fueled the fire.

"Disgusting!" said Merriam Holt.

"Creepy." Said Shannon Portman.

Clyde Parsons chimed in, "He's got to be stopped, Sheriff, before something bad happens."

"To you or to him?" asked the sheriff.

"You know full well what I mean, Sheriff," Clyde said.

In fact, the sheriff didn't know what Clyde meant. These folks spooked too easily to actually go out in the woods and confront old Pete the hobo. That's why they came to him. They expected the sheriff to do their dirty work for them.

Sheriff Bryson asked the teacher, "Nell, do you have any proof?"

Mrs. Barker said, "You have my word, and that's all the proof you need."

The sheriff was treading on thin ice, and had to be careful how he handled the situation.

"Now Nell, you know I would never question your integrity, but it wasn't six weeks ago you claimed Preacher Smith was peeking in your window. Turns out, he was over at the V.A. hospital ministering to the veterans."

The teacher was adamant, "It *was* Preacher Smith, and I assure you."

"Nell, there were twenty witnesses at the hospital, and also remember that just this past winter you made the same allegation against Clyde here." The sheriff said pointing toward Clyde.

This seemed to knock some of the wind out of her sail as Clyde stared at her in disbelief. She said, "I know what I saw."

The sheriff placed one of his big hands on the teacher's dainty shoulder, and said soothingly, "Mrs. Barker, it was winter, there was four feet of snow. I tramped around your house for an hour that night, and didn't find one track or footprint. In fact I dang near froze my butt off and caught a heck of cold after that."

The crowd was subdued at this new bit of information and he took the opportunity to put an end to the protest.

"Now, why don't you folks go on home. I'll file a report that y'all made a complaint and I'll investigate it."

The crowd slowly shuffled towards the door, mumbling as they left the sheriff's office. Once they were gone he smiled and shook his head. Those people were his friends, but they sure could get worked up and bent out of shape now and then. He made a mental note to go out and have a word with Pete, the old hobo, as the town folk had dubbed him, the first chance he got. But there was no hurry. The Sheriff knew Pete well, and knew he would never stoop to the things he was accused of. Pete had problems that was for sure, but he was a man of honor and respect. And that was something the sheriff had witnessed firsthand.

Illustration 5: Hobo Pete Meets the Boys

CHAPTER 8

Hobo Pete was hiding behind a tree, watching the boys as they rode up on their bikes. It looked as if these boys were going to be around every day since summer was coming, and that just wouldn't do. These were his woods, and he didn't need any kids roaming around.

The place where he lived was a cave not far from where the boys had built their treehouse, and even though it was well hidden, Pete knew how curious and adventurous young boys could be.

He'd have to scare them off, that's all there was to it. But he'd have to be careful how he did that. If the boys suspected him, instead of some bear or bobcat, they'd be back with some town's people and flush him out.

Pete had heard the talk, Sheriff Bryson made sure of that. Folks said he was a murderer, an escaped convict, a no good thief, all of which were not true.

He had his reasons for living alone out in the woods, and only he knew why. Well, except for Sheriff Bryson, he knew why. After all, he and the sheriff had known each other all their lives.

Yes, he'd be careful not to scare the boys into thinking it was him, but he had to get rid of them.

Pete watched as the boys climbed the ladder to their treehouse. One of them, the taller one, was carrying a white paper sack. He wondered if there was food in that sack.

If it was food maybe they'd leave some of it behind. He decided to wait until they left, then climb the ladder and see.

Matt shut the door as soon as all three were inside, turned and said, "Let's eat."

I said, "Calm down, you'll get your share. Besides, you should go easy on these sweets or else Mom will have you drinking Castor Oil."

Matt and Ben were momentarily unable to speak, just the mention of Castor Oil has that effect on kids, me included.

I slowly opened the bag we'd picked up from the Duchess Bakery in town.

Carlton Morgan had owned the Duchess Bakery for longer than we have been alive. In fact the bakery had been in the Morgan family for seventy-five years and it was famous for miles around. Pastries that did not sell throughout the day were placed in a bag and sold at a discount just as school let out.

There was a mix of doughnuts, cookies and pastries, and you never knew what you might get. But one thing was for sure, whatever was in the bag, it was well worth the fifty cents you had to pay for it.

I peeked in the bag and said excitedly, "Well boys, we hit the jackpot today, look at what we got."

I ripped the bag open and spread the contents out on the paper. Matt and Ben's eyes bulged out of their heads.

Before us were chocolate covered doughnuts, cinnamon twists, oatmeal raisin cookies and best of all, a *Bizmark*.

We had no idea how the pastry got its name but the Bizmark was known far and wide.

It's a peculiar pastry shaped like a long john, or maybe a flat hot dog bun. There was a cut down the length of it and it actually opened up like a hot dog bun. There was no glaze or chocolate icing on the outside; it was rather plain looking, but inside was white cream along with vanilla pudding.

We were surprised there were any Bizmarks left to put in the after school grab bags since they were usually the first items sold in the mornings. We thought that Mr. Morgan saved some for us kids since he knew how much we enjoyed them.

"Okay boys, nobody touch the Bizmark, we'll save it 'til last and split it three ways. Now dig in."

We tore into the treats like one of those lions we'd seen on National Geographic mauling some gazelle he'd run down.

When we finished all the pastries except the Bizmark, I pulled my Old-Timer pocket knife from my jeans pocket and cut it into three pieces. Matt and Ben paid close attention making sure the portions were equal.

I was cleaning the knife and slipping it back into my pocket when Ben said, "Did y'all hear it?"

Matt and I knew he was referring to the Ghost Train. We both nodded and I said, "It was Toby's grandma. He wasn't in class today and Mrs. Collins told us."

Our moods were suddenly dampened by the thoughts of the Ghost Train and none of us was in a hurry to eat the Bizmark. Ben asked the same question we always asked the day after we heard the train. "Andy, why do we hear the Ghost Train and nobody else does?"

Matt chimed in, "And why do people die when we hear it?"

They were staring at me, waiting for answers. After all, I was older and in middle school, so I should have the answers, right? Well the truth was, I didn't have any answers. I did have a theory though, but that's all it was … a theory. I said, "The only thing I can think of is this, the train must be picking up the souls of dead people. It must have been sent to pick them up."

Ben said, "That don't make no kinda sense, Andy. Besides, we're the only ones who hear it, remember?"

Matt joined in, "Yeah Andy, why doesn't anybody else hear it?"

"How do you know nobody else hears it?" I asked. "What if the people who died heard it?"

They sat in silence for a moment, deep in thought. Finally Matt said, "If the people who died heard it before they died, then you know what that means ... right?"

I asked, "What Matt, what does it mean?"

"It means we're going to die Andy, that's what."

As much as I hated to admit it, Matt's theory had as much merit to it as mine. I didn't want to talk about it anymore. It was getting too depressing, and I certainly didn't want to think Matt's theory might have some truth to it.

"Listen you two numb-skulls, if I knew why the Ghost Train only comes when people die I'd tell you, but I don't, and I ain't about to go around asking folks either. Next thing you know, they'd have us in the looney bin. Is that what y'all want?"

Matt and Ben hung their heads and mumbled in unison, "No."

"Well good, now let's eat this here Bizmark, unless of course, y'all are too upset to eat your share in which case I'd have it all to myself.

They were reaching for their slice of the Bizmark when we heard the noise just outside the treehouse door.

WE FROZE!

CHAPTER 9

For the longest time we sat in silence, afraid to breathe. After not hearing anything for a few minutes, I moved slowly toward the door, gently put my hand on the latch, then turned to look at Matt and Ben ... you could see they were scared.

With a hard push I flung the door open, it caught on something momentarily then flew wide open. We saw him just before he disappeared. That dirty old hobo had been standing at the top of the ladder and when I shoved the door open it knocked him off.

We heard him grunting as he hit a couple of limbs on his way down, and there was a loud thump as he finally landed on the ground.

We were lying on the floor, side by side, staring down at the hobo below. He didn't appear to be breathing and his arms and legs were crooked looking.

Matt whispered, "Do you think he's dead?"

Ben said, "He looks dead to me."

"How would you know stupid, have you ever seen a real live dead person?" I asked.

Ben replied, "How can a real live person be dead?"

I rolled my eyes and said, "You know what I mean."

Matt said, "He ain't movin', he's got to be dead. Gollee Andy, you killed a man and you ain't even in high school yet!"

"Shut up, I ain't killed nobody," I exclaimed.

"Well, he sure looks dead to me Andy."

"Stop saying that, he's probably just knocked out or something."

Matt said, "You better hope so. You know they execute murderers in this state."

"I ain't killed nobody, all I did was open the door and he fell!"

"More like you knocked him off the ladder," said Ben.

"Yeah," Matt joined in, "and now he's dead."

Boy, these guys were brutal! It's a good thing they weren't old enough to be on jury duty or else I'd be a goner for sure.

Ben said, "Go check on him Andy, we'll stay up here and guard the treehouse."

There was no need to argue with them, I'd be wasting my breath. I shook my head and said, "Geez, a couple of girls, that's what y'all are."

I climbed slowly down the ladder all the while keeping a close eye on the hobo; he still hadn't moved and I was starting to think that maybe he *was* dead. When I made it to the ground I moved towards him on shaky legs. I found a stick lying close by and picked it up. Standing directly over the hobo, the smell hit me like a skillet to the face. Man, did he stink! I covered my nose and poked him in the ribs with the stick... nothing happened. He still wasn't moving, I poked a little harder, but he still showed no signs of life. I turned to look up at Matt and Ben and shrugged my shoulders not knowing what to do next.

Matt asked, "Is he dead? Check his pulse."

Ben said, "Check his breathing."

Boy for a couple of scaredy cats, those two sure had a lot of suggestions. But maybe I should check his breathing, if I could stand the smell that is.

I dropped down on one knee beside him and the smell got stronger.

Geez I thought, when was the last time this guy had a bath?

Almost vomiting I put my ear close to his mouth to see if I could hear any breathing. I really couldn't tell. I thought about raising one of his eyelids to see what I could see.

I held a hand just above his face and was about to raise an eyelid when suddenly both of the hobo's eyes flew wide open and he was staring right at me. He shouted, "Boo!" and I just about peed my pants right there on the spot.

I fell backwards and scrambled on my hands and knees as fast as I could until I was at the bottom of the ladder.

I heard Ben shout, "Run Andy, he's getting up!"

On my first attempt to scale the ladder, I failed miserably – for the life of me I could not get a foot hold on the ladder.

Matt screamed, "He's coming after you!" That did it. Without looking back, I scrambled up the ladder in record time. Once inside the treehouse I said breathlessly, "Shut the door!"

We could hear the old hobo laughing and coughing at the same time, and it made an eerie sound. But he wouldn't stop; his wheezing seemed to be haunting us.

Finally the laughing stopped and I said, "See if he's still there, Ben."

Ben peeked through a hole we'd drilled in the door, "Yep, he's still there."

We heard him cough and start to laugh again as we inched towards the door and cracked it open just enough for the three of us to look outside.

The hobo was standing at the bottom of the ladder, looking up at us. I was shaking like a leaf and I was sure we were goners. I said the one thing I thought might save us from the 'Butcher', as the town folks liked to call him, "I'm sorry, Mister, I didn't mean to hurt you. It was an accident. Now can you please go away?"

He just laughed again, so I tried a different tactic. "My Dad's on his way, he's gonna be here any minute, you better go before he gets here. He's big and mean, and he won't like you scaring us like this."

There was more laughing and coughing. When he calmed down he said, "Your pa ain't comin' and besides, I've seen him, he ain't no taller than me and he's skinny."

So this was it, we were all about to die at the hands of Hobo Pete, that murdering crazy man who lived in the woods.

To my horror Matt started whimpering and said, "Please Mister, don't eat us."

Hobo Pete doubled over laughing and I thought he might actually cough up a lung. He said, "Well now that you mention it, I am kinda hungry."

Ben said, "Holy crap Matt, why'd you have to go and remind him?"

The old man looked up at us and said, "Tell you what boys, y'all let me have that Bizmark and I'll leave y'all alone."

We breathed a sigh of relief. It looked like we were going to make it out of this alive, and all it was going to cost us was our Bizmark.

I shouted down to him, "Okay Mister, here it comes."

After wrapping the Bizmark in the paper bag I tossed it down to him. He caught it and tore into the Bizmark like he was starving, and maybe he was.

Nothing was said until he'd finished devouring the creamy treat.

Then he looked up at us and said, "Thanks boys, I haven't had a Bizmark in years. They're still as good as ever."

I was surprised to learn that the old hobo knew about the Bizmark but was happy he enjoyed it and was finished. I said, "Okay Mister, can you please go now?"

Hobo Pete looked up at us boys but he wasn't smiling

anymore. His face had grown serious looking. He said, "Okay boys, a deal is a deal, you gave me the Bizmark so I'll go now. But... if I go, you may never know the answer to your question."

I said, "What question is that mister?"

"Why you hear the Ghost Train." He said as he turned to walk away.

We were shocked to say the least. For the first time we'd found someone else who knew about the Ghost Train.

I called after him, "Hey Mister, wait. How do you know about the Ghost Train?"

He stood there staring up at us for the longest time. Then he answered, "Because I hear it, too."

Finally maybe we would learn the secret of the Ghost Train. I asked, "Can you tell us why we hear it when nobody else does."

Matt, Ben and I lay there on the floor of the treehouse, our heads hanging through the door, waiting for an answer.

What he said next chilled us to the bone.

"It means you're gonna die."

Illustration 6: Platform in Hobo Pete's Dreams

CHAPTER 10

Hobo Pete was sitting cross legged on the floor of our treehouse. He was in one corner and we were huddled together in the opposite corner. We stared at him, still frightened to be so close to the "Butcher". I noticed he still had some cream from the Bizmark stuck in his beard, and boy, did he stink. I wanted to know about the Ghost Train but Matt had to go and open his mouth about a different subject. He said, "Gollee Mister, when was the last time you had a bath?"

I elbowed Matt hard in the ribs, "Shut up, stupid!" Man, I thought, what was he trying to do, get us killed?

Hobo Pete raised an arm and sniffed his armpit. He shrugged his shoulders and said, "I don't know, maybe a day or two."

Matt opened his mouth to say something else, but I jabbed him again, stopping him before he could make another stupid comment. We were all thinking the same thing. It had been more than a day or two since the old man had taken a bath. I was betting it was more like a year or two.

I didn't care, I just wanted to know about the Ghost Train. "Mister, how do you know we're gonna die just because we hear the train?"

He stared at us for the longest time and finally said, "How long you boys been hearing the train?"

"About a month now." I answered "We all hear it, but nobody else does."

"As far as you know, nobody else hears it," he said.

Hobo Pete lowered his head and nodded as if he'd just gotten the answer to a question. He continued, "And I believe I overheard you say that every time you hear the train, someone dies?"

We nodded in unison, not really wanting to talk about the dead. We were scared and confused.

He sensed our confusion and said, "Listen boys, I don't know all the answers myself, but things are getting a little clearer since I met y'all. Let me tell you about the dreams I've been having. I've been having these terrible dreams for a long time now and up until recently they'd always been the same. In the dream I'd be walking and I'd always end up in the same place. There's this platform in the woods where I would go to in my dreams. And every time I stepped onto the platform, a train would pass by right in front of me."

We sat there silent with our eyes wide open, hanging on every word the old hobo had to say. He would pause occasionally, but eventually he'd continue with his story.

"The train seemed to glide across the top of the ground. I could see right through it and the people too. There were lots of passengers on board but they were all dead. The passengers, *and* the train, were ghosts. The train never stopped, it just passed slowly by then disappeared into the foggy night. As it disappeared, I saw this evil looking conductor standing at the door of the last car. He would stare at me with these red eyes, and smile. Anyway, like I said, that's how the dreams had always been up until about a month ago. But then the dreams changed, and after hearing you boys talk about the train, I think I know what's happening."

I asked, "What is it Mister, what do you think is happening, why do we hear the train?"

Hobo Pete said, "I'm not positive what's happening, but I'm starting to put the pieces of the puzzle together. You see, about a month ago, about the same time y'all starting hearing the train, my dreams changed. The train and the conductor were still in my dreams but somehow the dream seemed more... real. It was pretty cold that night and I had a fire going. But sometime during the night, the fire burned out. I was too cold to get out from underneath the covers to get it started up again, so I just lay there in my cave, staring into the darkness."

The old man had a faraway look in his eyes as he continued and we sat and listened, unable to speak, almost unable to breathe.

"At first I thought I was awake, but I wasn't. It was a dream and something from the darkness seemed to be calling me, pulling me from my blankets almost. The next thing I knew I was walking through the woods. But not really, I was just dreaming, or maybe it was real, I don't even know for sure. All I know is I could hear leaves crackling under my feet, and my breathing was loud. I could see my breath as clear as I can see you boys right now. But that was the only sounds. No critters moving about. No wind blowing through the trees. Complete silence was all there was. Though it was dark, I walked through the forest like I knew where I was going, like I'd been down the path before, until finally I came to a clearing and there it was."

Until then we'd been silent, but the old man was telling the story way too slowly for us. Matt said, "What was it Mister, what was there?"

"The platform I'd seen before in my dreams."

Ben asked, "What kind of platform Mister?"

"The kind you see in train stations. Only this one was small, maybe six feet by six feet. And next to it was a single light post, with an eerie glow around it. The strange thing was that was it, there was nothing else around… just the light and the platform, no building, no roads or tracks. How the light shone without electricity, I don't know. All of a sudden it got colder. Colder than before, and the thing that had seemed to be pulling me, now wanted me to step up on the platform. I couldn't actually hear a voice, or feel anything pushing or pulling me. It was more like it was in my head, but I didn't seem to have any control over myself. And for some reason I knew I had to step onto the platform, though I was afraid of what would happen if I did. When I did step onto the platform the light suddenly grew brighter and that's when I heard it."

Hobo Pete rested a moment before continuing. We'd been hanging on every word, but to tell the truth, we weren't so sure we wanted to hear the rest of the story. But we did. We had to know, because we were part of it.

Like I said boys, there were no tracks but I heard the train whistle as clear as a bell. At first I couldn't tell from which direction the whistle came. I looked all around. Directly in front of me was a hill that rose up sharply about three hundred feet. To my left and right all I could see was the rounded curve that was the base of the hill. The fog got thicker and I heard it again. Only louder this time. It was getting closer. I tried to turn and run but I couldn't move. As the whistle got louder I realized it wasn't a whistle at all, it was more like a scream. In fact, it sounded like lots of people screaming all at once. There were dozens of them, maybe even hundreds.

A bright flashing light appeared through the fog to my right and I covered my ears to drown out the screaming. The rumbling of the engines sounded like a long thunderclap and it was deafening. I had my eyes closed tightly as the train pulled to a stop at the platform. A smell hit me that made me sick. It was strange that I could smell something in a dream. That's why I'm not so sure it was a dream. Anyway, the smell was horrible. It wasn't a smoke or diesel fuel smell, it was much worse, if I had to describe what the smell was I'd have to say it was ... the smell of death."

Illustration 7: The Evil Conductor

CHAPTER 11

Young boys will ask stupid question, that's for sure. But every now and then we ask good ones. Ben asked Hobo Pete, "How do you know what death smells like Mister?"

"Because I've smelled it before." He replied. "Dead burnt bodies, lying in a heap by the hundreds. That's the effects of war boys, and I hope you never have to experience it, but most likely you will. Anyway, that's a whole different nightmare."

We could sense he wanted to finish his story about the dream so we held our questions after that.

"When the screaming stopped I slowly opened my eyes and uncovered my ears. The horror that was before me was worse than anything I'd seen. A big dark train sat right there. It was dark, but at the same time it was transparent. I could see right through it. In fact I could see the passengers on it. They were all sitting in their seats talking to one another. But they were transparent too. God how I wanted to run away, to run as fast as I could from the nightmare. I desperately tried to will myself to turn and flee, but I couldn't. Then a door to one of the passenger cars opened. I stood there scared and waiting. A man in a conductor's uniform stepped through the door and looked down at me. He pulled a gold watch on a chain from his vest pocket and checked the time. He was also transparent and after he studied his watch for what seemed an eternity, he said in a deep voice, "Will you be boarding with us tonight sir?"

I couldn't move or speak. The conductor's eyes seemed on fire as he stared at me without blinking. The conductor continued, "Sir, time is wasting" My heart was about to explode out of my chest. Then he stepped down to the last step of the car, but would not step completely off the train. The smell of death was so strong I was nauseous. I could smell his awful breath as he said to me, "Sir, why don't you come aboard now, your family is waiting for you. In my dream I could feel tears rolling down my cheeks, and for the first time I was able to speak. I said to the conductor, "M-my family?"

The conductor said to me, "Sir, you owe us a fare. You purchased a ticket with this company and we pride ourselves on insuring our passengers arrive to their final destination on time. You are causing us to be late. Now, come aboard!" I shook my head, knowing that if I stepped on that train, there'd be no coming back. The conductor was furious with me now. He leaned closer to me and sneered, "Don't you want to be with your family. Don't you miss them? Your wife and children miss you. Now step aboard and be with them. They are waiting."

I gotta tell you boys, I was tempted, but I found the strength to say "no". This caused the conductor to explode in a fit of rage. He shouted at me, "Sir you have purchased a ticket with this company. You owe us a fare and you are causing us to be late, and we are always on time!"

I said to the conductor, "I can't do it" My voice was so soft I could barely hear myself.

He stood over me from his perch on the steps of the passenger car and his demeanor changed. Now he was smiling and soft spoken. He said, "Well... perhaps we can find another passenger to take your place. Is that what you want? Someone else to fill your seat on this train?"

At first I didn't understand what he was saying. But then it hit me, if I boarded the train I would surely be dead. But if I didn't, someone else would die.

As the conductor was about to step back into the car he looked over his shoulder at me and said, "Say goodbye to your family sir, and go back to that cave you've been living in. We'll find someone to take your place. Maybe even someone your children would enjoy for company."

And just like that the train sped away into the fog. The screaming was louder than before, but just as a passenger car near the end passed me by, I saw them. There looking out the window at me was my wife, daughter and son. They were crying and as I reached a hand out towards them my daughter raised a little gloved hand and waved goodbye to me.

I was crying so hard under the now dim light above the platform, I could barely make out the conductor's face as he stood at the door of the last passenger car and stared out the window at me."

One last time the conductor smiled, and shouted, "All Abooooard!"

We were scared to death and Hobo Pete was sobbing and mumbling incoherently.

With a trembling voice I said, "P-please Mister, tell us. Do you think the dream means the Ghost Train is coming after one of us now?"

Pete looked at me through tearful eyes and nodded.

It was so quiet in the treehouse you could have heard a pin drop. Then all of sudden, Ben broke wind. And I ain't talking about your normal fart. This one was long and loud. It reminded me of a cow bellowing.

We all stared at him in disbelief, and he said, "Sorry, but I always fart when I'm scared."

Then it hit us, the most God-awful smell we'd ever smelled. "Oh my God, Ben." I said as I buried my face into my t-shirt.

We scrambled for the door when we couldn't take it anymore, and to my surprise, Pete was the first one out the door. Boy, for an old guy, he sure could move.

After hitting the ground and taking a deep breath of fresh air I looked in Ben's direction and said, "Boy, you need help.

I'm gonna tell my Mom to give you some Castor Oil when we get home."

Ben said, "Awe come on Andy, it wasn't that bad. Besides, like I said, I was scared. It wasn't my fault."

Matt, who was standing a safe distance from Ben, said, "I've got to admit, I'm kinda scared too Andy. I think that Ghost Train is coming after one of us, and most likely it's me."

This comment silenced us. Who could dispute what Ben was saying?

Pete didn't know about Ben's condition, so he was confused. He looked at Ben and said, "What's wrong boy, why would he think it's you the train's coming after?"

CHAPTER 12

We were visibly shaken by the dream, and Pete wanted to tell us everything was going to be okay, but the truth was, Pete wasn't even sure himself.

Ben's voice was barely audible and he said, "I've got a weak heart."

Pete didn't understand at first. He just sat there in silence, staring at the boy waiting for more.

Ben explained, "The doctors say I was born with a weak heart and it has to work too hard to keep up. They say if I don't get a transplant, I'll die." He thought for a second then added, "They don't know how long I have."

The mood had gotten somber, and Andy felt he had to say something. "Don't worry Ben, you'll get a heart, I'm sure of it. And soon too."

Andy's words of encouragement didn't help much. Ben said what everyone had been thinking, "Maybe it is me the Ghost Train is coming after, and maybe my times almost up."

There were just too many strange things going on, what with the dream and us hearing the train. There had to be a logical answer to it all, and Ben's theory that the train was coming after him because he had a weak heart didn't explain why other people died when we heard the train. Pete offered another theory.

"Listen boys, I've been doing some thinking. You say every time you hear the train someone dies, right? Well think about it, there has to be more than one train because the one that comes to me in my dreams only has one vacant seat, and that's my seat, according to the conductor."

Matt blurted out, "Yeah, but if you don't get on that train, that conductor is gonna take somebody else in your place. Maybe that somebody is Ben."

The tears welled up in Matt's eyes as he made his thoughts known. Pete looked each of us in the eyes and could see all of us were scared. And we wanted Pete to help us make some sense of it all.

Pete explained, "Who's to say Ben has to ride on *that* train. Maybe all three of you will ride a train one day, but none of us know when our time's up. What if Ben gets a heart and lives forever? What if it's one of you two who dies? We just don't know."

Pete's explanation didn't do much to ease our minds. If anything, it only clouded matters more.

Matt had another thought, "But what about the fact that we all started hearing the train about the same time you first had your dream?"

It was a good point, but it was all just too complicated to explain. Pete made a feeble attempt to further explain, "It doesn't mean Ben is going to die, or any of us for that matter. Remember, it's still just a dream."

We no more believed that it was just a dream than Pete did. The fact was, people had died when we heard the train. And most times, we had been awake when we heard it. It was no dream that was for certain.

The mood had gotten too depressing for Pete. He needed to do something to take everybody's mind off the Ghost Train.

He said, "Hey, do you boys like to fish?"

Like a switch that had been flipped we went from sad to happy in the blink of an eye.

Pete smiled back at us and said, "Well, today's your lucky day, because I just happen to have a secret fishin' hole ... there's so many fish you get five fish on one hook."

I said, "But mister, we don't have any fishin' equipment."

"That's okay; I've got some cane poles and know where to dig us up some worms. We don't need nothing else."

We whooped and hollered as Pete said, "Follow me."

They were all so happy to have their minds on something other than the Ghost Train. But they all knew it would be back.

CHAPTER 13

Despite what we thought about Pete's dream and what it may or may not mean, we still liked him. Maybe it was because he was different, or maybe because they shared a common bond. To our knowledge, we were the only ones who heard the Ghost Train. During the coming weeks, Matt, Ben, and I would hang out in the treehouse every chance we got, and little by little we brought items that made the fort more complete.

There were a couple of folding lawn chairs we'd found thrown away; with a little mending, they worked perfectly. And Ben's Mom had even contributed an old rug that fit just right inside the treehouse. Pete brought a frying pan and an old coffee pot. He showed us how to clean fish, and cook them in the pan. We even had a pact that no girls were allowed and no one other than the three of us and Pete would ever be a part of the group.

Pete was enjoying every minute of the camaraderie. We would sneak him food from our houses, when we were sure our Moms wouldn't miss it, and about once a week, we'd bring a grab bag full of goodies from the Duchess Bakery.

On more than one occasion, we brought bars of soap

for Pete, but he would just sniff it, turn up his nose, and hand it back, as he shook his head.

We guessed he thought the smell of the soap was repulsive. Go figure!

Pete knew the woods well and would take us on long hikes through the Appalachians without so much as a map or compass. And just as easy as you please, he'd have us back to the treehouse before dark.

I'll tell you, we'd seen some pretty country on our hikes with Pete, country we'd never seen before.

On these jaunts through the hills, we saw plenty of wildlife too, like a family of black bears near a creek. There were lots of deer and red-tailed hawks about, but my favorite sighting was the day we stood on a rocky cliff and watched a bald eagle with its young at its wing teaching it how to soar.

Pete showed us snakes, vermin, and plants, both good and bad, and advised which ones to stay away from. One day, while he was showing the difference between poison oak and poison ivy, Pete found a sassafras plant that he tugged on and uprooted. He hacked off the roots and discarded the tree. Pete held the roots out for us to smell, just like root beer, we thought.

Back at the treehouse, be cleaned the roots then set them to boil in a pot of water. After straining the darkened water from the roots and adding sugar we'd swiped from home, he stirred it up real good and gave us all a cupful.

We sipped it slowly at first but as it cooled we quickly drained our cups and held them out for more. Pete smiled and explained to us that the sassafras root was used in the old days to make root beer. That's how it got its name.

The time we shared with Pete, albeit short-lived, was an invaluable experience to us boys. The things he taught us have stuck with me throughout my entire life.

We used to let Pete sleep in our treehouse. His cave didn't sound too comfortable, though we'd never seen it. Certainly the treehouse was better, we guessed.

We were okay with Pete sleeping in our treehouse. After all, he was one of us, although it took an hour to get the smell out. And that was with the doors and windows open.

Pete was good to us boys and not at all like the town people made him out to be. He wasn't a bad person, just different.

He never spoke about his family, and we never asked. We figured it was none of our business, and if he wanted us to know, then he'd tell us. But we agreed that he was from around the area since he knew the terrain so well.

To say Hobo Pete was our friend would be an understatement. Never had we boys met anyone like him before or since.

Looking back, I wish we could have known him better. But as it turns out, fate had other plans.

Illustration 8: The Angry Conductor

CHAPTER 14

Pete had fallen asleep thinking about the boys. He enjoyed their company and his missing his own children helped fill that void. It had been a long time since he'd been that close to anyone. Except the Sheriff of course. Allowing himself to become so close to the boys had caused him to become an emotional wreck though, part of him looked forward to their being around but another part of him wanted to run away. The last he remembered was staring into his campfire and thinking about them before he dozed off. But sometime during the night the fire had gone out and he came awake with a jerk, suddenly trembling and afraid. Then he realized he wasn't awake at all. It was the dream again. There was absolute silence and before him was the wooden platform and flickering light post. Without taking a step or making a move he was suddenly standing on the platform. Then came the screaming whistle of the Ghost Train. It was coming. The louder the whistle became, the brighter the light got. Then suddenly, it was there before him.

The dream seemed to be moving in fast-forwarded clips. First he was through the woods in a clip. Then onto the platform. And now the train was before him.

He stood frozen in place on the platform as a door opened on the passenger car before him. The Conductor stepped out, pulled his gold watch from his pocket and checked the time. Then, with an evil look, he said to Pete in that menacing voice of his, "Are you boarding sir?" Pete only stared at the Ghostly Conductor, unable to move. "Sir, please step aboard, we have a schedule to keep." the Conductor said in a less menacing tone. Then he added, "Mr. Hanson, your family is waiting."

Pete started shaking uncontrollably as if he were freezing. He found himself raising a hand to the handrail. The he placed a foot on the first step of the passenger car. The Conductor smiled though his red eyes were pure evil, "Careful now. Watch your step, sir." The Conductor held out a white gloved hand to Pete, but he couldn't take it. In fact, he found the strength to release the handrail and step backwards onto the platform. This infuriated the Conductor and he lunged for Pete, but stopped himself short of stepping off the train. No, he couldn't do that. He roared at Pete, "DO YOU KNOW WHAT YOU'VE DONE? YOU'VE COST THIS RAIL COMPANY VALUABLE TIME AS IT IS!"

Pete was in tears. The Conductor had frightened him and that was not an easy thing to do.

The Conductor went from being angry to jovial and smiling in the blink of an eye. He stared down at Pete and again he checked his watch. "Oh my, look at the time. We are running late, late, late."

As Pete stood listening and watching the Conductor, the rail man added, "I'm afraid it's a little late for you as well, Mr. Hanson. You've missed this train." Another fast forward clip and the train was disappearing around the bend into the cloud of fog. The Conductor was standing looking out the door of the last passenger car. The light grew dim and flickered as he heard the Conductor's voice from the fog.

"AAALLLL Abooooard! HA, HA, HA, HA."

Pete woke up inside his cave and swore he could hear the Conductor's laugh echoing through the cave. He sat up straight and realized he was sweating through his clothes, and said, "Noooooooo!" Then he fell back onto his dirty blankets and began to sob. Pete had not cried or felt this way since his family died. The pain was unbearable.

Illustration 9: Julie Working at Taylor's Grocery

CHAPTER 15

School was less than a week away from summer recess. I was looking forward to spending as much time as I could with Maryanne, so, there I was, standing at the entrance of her father's store, Taylor's Grocery.

Applying for my first job was a big event, and I had talked it over with my Dad. I kinda wanted him to come along because I was a little nervous, but he said it was best if I went alone. He explained that going alone would give the appearance of being someone who could stand on his own.

Dad also gave advice on how best to approach Mr. Taylor for the job. I would need to convince Mr. Taylor that I was reliable, honest, and a hard worker, in addition to being a fast learner.

It all sounded good coming out of my Dad's mouth, but I had no idea how I was supposed to relay all that to Mr. Taylor. It was a lot to remember for such a young boy as myself.

Dad knew what I was thinking and with a smile he said, "Just tell the truth, son, everything else will fall into place."

I nodded and then thought about the real reason I was applying for the job. Working for Mr. Taylor would give me more opportunities to see Maryanne. All in all, it was a lot of pressure just to get close to a girl. But I had a feeling she was worth it. I have to admit, there was a moment there I thought about turning away. But I knew I had to give it a try. So I took a deep breath then stepped inside Taylor's Grocery Store.

There were two checkout counters but only one was occupied by an employee. The girl behind the counter was Julie Burgess. Julie was 18 at the time and I knew her well. She'd babysat Matt and I years before but I hadn't seen her in some time. When I walked to the checkout counter, Julie was bagging a customer's groceries. I stood and waited until she was finished.

Julie had grown quite a bit since I'd last seen her. She had her dark hair pulled back into a ponytail and her bangs were cut straight across her forehead at eyebrow level. She wore tight fitting blue jeans with the cuff rolled up to mid-calf, a pair of white, low-cut tennis shoes and a floral, button-up blouse. Over her attire was a white apron with "Taylor's Grocery" embroidered across the front. Also there was a plastic name tag pinned to the apron with her name carved into it.

She caught a glimpse of me standing and said, "Hi Andy." Her lips were painted bright red and she had what had to be a whole pack of bubble gum in her mouth, which she chomped on with due diligence. Julie had the gum on the side of her mouth and this caused her cheek to bulge abnormally. She bagged the customer's groceries and asked if they needed help carrying them and when they declined she thanked them in a voice that was as unemotional and mechanical as a robot.

With the customer gone, Julie turned and said, "So, how's it going Andy? I ain't seen you in a while. How's your brother?" Then she blew a huge bubble with her gum until it popped and covered half her face.

I smiled and said, "Hey that was a big one!"

She smiled and shrugged her shoulders like it was no

big deal.

"I'm okay Julie. So's Matt. I'm in middle school now."

"My, my, how the time flies. I remember when you weren't even in school yet." She said standing there with one hand on a hip the other playing with her hair, and her mouth smacking away at the gum.

I was nervous thinking about what I was going to say to Mr. Taylor, and Julie didn't help any. Older girls make me jittery.

"Is Mr. Taylor here?"

"He's in the storeroom. Just go on back. It's okay."

I mumbled, "Thanks," and headed towards the back of the store.

Julie, suspecting why I was there, called after me, "If you're looking for a job, Bo Barnette done beat ya to it. He was in here earlier."

That news hit me like a rock, I had to admit. I almost turned and walked out. How could I possibly compete with Bo Barnette? Bo was tall, strong, and good looking. Surely Mr. Taylor had already given the job to Bo. What Mr. Taylor didn't know though, was that Bo was rotten to the core. He was a bully. I'd lost count of how many windows he'd knocked out around town, and I knew he even drowned a cat once. It was a neighbor's cat, and Bo had tied one end of a rope to a cinder block and the other end around the cat's neck, then threw them both into a pond. And the worst part was, he never got caught. Everything always got blamed on someone else. The town folk would say that there was no way it could have been Bo, he was just too handsome.

It made me want to vomit. All my life I never hated anybody, except Bo Barnett. Well, maybe hate is too strong of a word. Despise might be more appropriate. Either way, my stomach took a flip at the thought of Bo Barnett working for Mr. Taylor, the father of Maryanne.

I found Mr. Taylor in the storeroom just like Julie said I would. He was marking prices on some canned peaches when he noticed me walking up. "Hey young fella, you lost?"

Mr. Taylor was a round, portly-looking man with a bald head and a double chin that jiggled when he talked. He wore brown, loose-fitting slacks, plain-looking brown shoes with soft soles and a plaid shirt. Like Julie, he wore the same apron and his name tag said, "Wesley."

I said, "No sir. My name's Andy Lockhart and I wanted to apply for a job."

Mr. Taylor went back to marking the cans and kinda looked at me out of the corner of his eyes as he said, "I'm sorry son, you're a little late. That opening was filled just this morning."

My head dropped. Dang that Bo Barnett. He'd stolen my job, and most likely he'd steal my girl before all was said and done. I took it hard but there was nothing I could do or say, so I just turned to walk away. My heart was sinking.

Mr. Taylor said, "That's all you got? Just turn and leave. You're not much of a fighter are you?"

I was confused. What did he expect? The job was Bo's and there was nothing left to do or say. Then I thought about what he'd said. Maybe Bo didn't have the job sewed up just yet and he wanted to hear what I had to offer. Maybe there was still a chance.

Holding nothing back I said, "Mr. Taylor, I ain't never worked in a grocery store before. Heck, I ain't never worked anywhere, except around the yard at home. But my Dad ain't never complained."

He stood with his hands on his hips listening to me as I continued. "Sir, I'll work hard, learn the job and do anything you ask me to here at the store. And I don't care how much you pay me, in fact, I'll work for free. Just don't give the job to Bo Barnett. He ain't like you think. He's rotten I tell you. I know firsthand."

I was out of breath and was about to go on when Mr. Taylor said, "You shouldn't talk bad about people who ain't around to defend themselves."

"I know, Mr. Taylor, but if Bo were here, I'd say it to his face. I ain't scared of him like some folks are. He's got the whole town fooled. He ain't what you think."

Mr. Taylor covered his mouth and appeared to be in deep thought, but I couldn't help but notice a smile behind his hand.

I said, "Mr. Taylor, give me a chance. You won't regret it. I'll be here every day and you won't ever hear me complain. I'm strong for a boy my age, and I'm smart too."

Mr. Taylor asked, "Are Linda and Robert Lockhart your parents?"

"Yes sir," I replied with a lump in my throat.

He said, "When can you start?"

I was so excited I almost choked, "Right now! I can start now!"

He smiled, held out his hand and said, "Congratulations, you're hired."

I reached out and shook his hand like a real grown up shaking on an agreement to some big business deal. And actually, it *was* a big deal. That job with Mr. Taylor played an important part in shaping my future.

Mr. Taylor got serious then, and said, "Okay, the job pays fifty cents an hour. You'll have to stock shelves, bag groceries, make deliveries occasionally, and help clean up. Think you can handle that?"

"You bet I can!" I half shouted.

"Okay then, grab a broom and let's get this storeroom cleaned up. You're on the clock as of right now."

I spotted a broom and mop in a corner and ran towards them. A thought occurred to me and I stopped and turned to Mr. Taylor.

"What's the matter?" he asked.

"Mr. Taylor. What about Bo?"

"Well, until you showed up, Bo Barnett was the only one who'd applied. I hire people based on how they present themselves. I feel like this business suits you better than him. So I'm choosing you over him. And besides," he said, "Us town folk ain't as easily fooled as some might think. We know all about Bo Barnett and the things he's done."

We stood there smiling at each other for a moment. So, the grown-ups weren't fooled by Bo's antics? I never would have guessed it.

He said gruffly, "Well, you gonna stand there all day with that funny looking grin on your face, or are you gonna do some work?"

I swept floors, took out the trash and even got a lesson in bagging groceries. Milk and canned goods on the bottom, eggs and bread on the top. Sometimes double bag, and never, never overload.

Three hours later Mr. Taylor handed me a daily work schedule and told me I'd done enough for one day and sent me home.

On my way out the door I bumped into Maryanne. "I'm sorry. I wasn't watching where I was going."

When she smiled at me, I swear I was looking into the eyes of an angel.

"So, did you get the job?" she asked

"Yeah, your Dad chose me over Bo Barnett." I answered, my chest swelling as I said it.

"Good choice. My Daddy's a pretty smart man. So, I guess I'll be seeing you around here a little more often?"

"I guess. Well bye, Maryanne. It's good talking to you."

"You too, Andy. See you later." She turned and walked into the store.

I felt great! Life was good.

Illustration 10: Andy Sees Maryanne as an Angel

CHAPTER 16

"Mr. and Mrs. Gordon," the pretty blonde assistant said as she stepped into the waiting room, "the doctor will see you now."

Walter and Carole Gordon had been sitting in the waiting room for only minutes, but it had seemed an eternity.

Doc Martin, as he was more affectionately known around town, was Ben's family doctor and he'd called the Gordons in for a consultation. Instinctively, the Gordons suspected the news would not be good. Still, they were hopeful.

Doc Martin stepped from behind the desk as his assistant led them into his office. He extended his hand, "Thank you for coming on such short notice."

Walter said, "We will always be available as long as Benjamin needs us. I hope everything is okay, Doc."

Doc Martin had a concerned, sad look on his face, "Please, have a seat." He motioned to the leather chairs positioned in front of his desk.

Carol Gordon had not spoken a word since arriving at the Doctor's office. Now she sat in silence, almost holding her breath, anticipating the terrible news that was about to come. She had a white handkerchief in her hands and she was inadvertently wringing it so tightly that her knuckles were pale and colorless.

Doc Martin hated this part of his profession more than anything. The bearer of bad news. The Grim Reaper. And when children were involved, it made it even worse.

One constant he'd learned during his career was that people wanted to hear it straight, be the news good or bad. They wanted honesty. That considered, he clenched his jaw and said, "I'm afraid Ben's latest test results are not that good."

Carol exhaled with a whimper and started to cry. Walter pulled her to him and she buried her face into his shoulder. He said in a voice that was trembling and barely audible, "Just give it to us straight, Doc. We're prepared for the worst."

And there it was. Honesty. Just give it to them straight. My God, how could anyone prepare themselves to lose a child? He was almost in tears himself.

His own voice cracked as he said, "The official version is that Ben's condition has deteriorated significantly since last we tested him. So much so that we have reached a point of diminishing returns regarding medications and treatment. In Layman's terms, Ben's not responding to medications, and as much as I hate to admit it ... the end is near."

Both of the Gordon's were crying now. Doc Martin continued, "There's still hope for a donor, but I'm afraid that's all that's left at this point."

Walter was able to find his voice and asked, "How long, Doc?"

Again Carol was holding her breath waiting for Doc Martin's verdict.

"Two, maybe three weeks at the most."

Carol lost it right then and there. She began sobbing uncontrollably, and as Walter tried to comfort her, he began weeping himself.

Doc Martin sat in silence, staring at nothing in particular on his desk, giving them enough time to come to grips with the prognosis. When he felt that enough time had passed, he said softly, "Folks, there's still hope for a donor. And when one comes through, we'll be ready to transport Ben to Cincinnati where the surgery will take place. It's only a thirty minute flight."

He continued, hoping talking might help, but not even sure the Gordon's heard a word he said, "Now, Ben's a strong boy. And, I've been informed that because of his condition, based on the latest test results, that he has been placed at the top of the list."

Walter tried to be strong. He held his head up and said, "What do you need us to do? What can we do?"

Doc Martin said, "Well, I want you to restrict Ben to your home. Keep a very close eye on him and don't allow him to get too excited. I'll be out to visit every day, and eventually we'll have to admit him to the hospital. "

There was more sobbing and Doc Martin searched for something to say, "Listen folks, Ben needs you two to be strong, now more than ever. So just go home and spend some time with him."

The crying subsided albeit slowly, and Doc Martin tried to imagine the pain they were feeling. It's one thing to have a loved one die suddenly, they're gone in an instant, you mourn and eventually you move on. However, it's an entirely different situation to sit for days, even weeks, and watch the one you love slowly fade away... especially if that loved one is a child.

You have time to think, and that's the worse part. You question God. Why the child, and not yourself? Then you think that somewhere someone has to die to save your child, and the whole time the clock is ticking at warp speed it seems.

No, Doc Martin could not imagine the grief the Gordons were going through. Oh, he'd seen his share of death and dying in his time. Far too much of it, and it was never easy. Now and again someone with Ben's condition would miraculously survive, but invariably more would die. One step forward, and two steps back. Doc Martin was lost in his own thoughts, and at first didn't hear Walter speaking to him, "I'm sorry Walter, what were you saying?"

Walter had always been a strong, vibrant man, but now he looked beaten and weak. He said in a barely audible voice, "Should we start making arrangements?"

So there it was. The ultimate question: when do you let go? Doc Martin couldn't count the times he had sat in that same office and been asked the same question.

He gave the question much thought, and like always, he was about to give it to them straight. Looking into the Gordons' eyes he just couldn't bring himself to do it. So for the first time in his life, he lied.

"You most certainly do not! Ben's going to get a heart. Now, I'm not going to give up on him. How about you folks?"

This stung the Gordons, but the Doc was right. Making arrangements would mean they'd resigned to Ben's not being around. It meant giving up.

Walter barely managed a thin smile and said with as much conviction as he could find, "We most certainly are not giving up on him, Doc. He is gonna make it and we're gonna be strong for him. Thank you, Doc."

They stood, and as Doc Martin walked them to the door he shook Walter's hand and gave Linda a hug, and said, "You folks call me the minute there's any change. I'll stop by tomorrow to check on him."

They nodded, and walked out without further conversation. When the door closed behind them, Doc Martin rested his head on it and closed his eyes. He was drained, both emotionally and physically.

Lying to people was not his way of doing business. But sometimes, one had to lie to keep people from thinking about the truth.

And the truth was, Ben had very little time left. Very little.

* * * * *

Walter helped Linda into the front passenger seat of their old Buick. After climbing behind the wheel, he hesitated for a full minute without starting the engine. Linda finally reached over and put a hand on his arm.

"Honey, let's go." She said with tears in her eyes.

Walter composed himself, started the engine and pulled out of the parking lot.

They were sitting at a red light just in front of Taylor's Grocery and Linda was staring out the passenger window, lost in thought, when he caught her eye. It was that old man who lived out in the woods, Hobo Pete, she remembered him being called.

He was climbing out of a dumpster with trash in his hand. She had been oblivious to everything around her until now. Why had the old bum caught her attention?

Pete had been scavenging for food or anything of value when something caused him to look at the woman sitting in the old Buick at the red light.

Linda had never given a second look at the man in the past, but now she was entranced with him as they locked eyes with each other. She'd been repulsed by the dirty old bum before but looking at him now, she was overcome with a feeling of warmth and comfort.

Pete stared back at the woman, and for reasons unknown to him, he raised his hand in a wave and nodded his head.

Linda Gordon smiled and touched the car window with her hand, almost as if reaching for the man. Tears flowed from her eyes, and they held each other's gaze until the man was out of sight.

Pete had never seen the woman before, and normally would not have locked eyes with the town folk. Still, he felt a strange connection to her, though he didn't know why.

CHAPTER 17

Robert Lockhart had worked at Carbon Hollow's only lumber yard for ten years. And during those ten years, he'd been coming home every day for lunch without missing a one. Today was no different, so at precisely 11:45 he pulled his old Chevy pickup into the drive of his house at 314 Maple Street.

Linda Lockhart was a miracle worker when it came to lunch made from leftovers. Most of the meals consisted of soup and sandwiches however, she was quite adept at serving lunches that never repeated.

Today was Robert's favorite, spaghetti sandwiches and minestrone soup. Spaghetti in the south differs a bit from the style used up north. Instead of the noodles being placed on a plate and the meat sauce poured over the top, Southerners mix the pasta and meat sauce together while cooking.

Leftover spaghetti is then placed in a bowl in the refrigerator and thickens as it sits. The next day the spaghetti is scooped out of the bowl and cooked in a frying pan.

Linda would make toast, place a helping of spaghetti onto it, cover it with sliced cheese or grated Parmesan and serve it with soup. Delicious!

Linda placed two thick spaghetti sandwiches and the soup on the table in front of Robert and returned to the kitchen for some sweet iced tea.

She called out from the kitchen, "We need to talk about them boys of yours."

Uh-oh, he thought, they must be in trouble. Whenever Andy and Matt do us proud they're her boys, or at the very least, our boys. But let them do something wrong and they were *my* boys.

Robert said, "By, 'my boys,' you actually mean our boys, right?" Silently, he was praying that whatever they'd done wouldn't be bad enough to ruin his lunch.

Linda walked from the kitchen with two glasses of tea in her hands and a scowl on her face. She sat at the table with him, "You know full well what I mean."

He just smiled and took a bite of his sandwich.

Linda said, "Well, there was another meeting last night at the Sheriff's off...?"

Robert interrupted, saying, "Oh, you mean the lynch mob?" He'd heard all about the crowd who'd rushed into Sheriff Bryson's office the night before and demanded again that the Sheriff arrest the old bum who lived in the woods.

To his recollection the man had never hurt anyone or stole anything. He pretty much stayed to himself, and for the life of him Robert couldn't understand why folks just didn't leave the man alone.

Linda didn't appreciate her husband's sarcasm, and she made it known with a glare. She said, "Be that as it may, I agree with them. There's something wrong with a man who lives in the woods and has no contact with people. Why, its plain scary!"

"Honey, he ain't bothering nobody. Why can't y'all just leave him alone? But to be honest, I wouldn't want any contact with the town people either, the way they're acting."

There was that glare again. She said, "Well, maybe the Sheriff won't do anything, but that doesn't mean we can't."

Robert stopped in mid-bite and stared at his wife.

All he wanted to do was enjoy his sandwich. Nothing more. Was that too much to ask? He said, "What do you plan to do about it? Have you been hittin' the cider again?"

This time he got the glare plus folded arms across her breast. "You know I don't drink. What I'm talking about is the fact that your boys spend an awful lot of time out in those woods, and I'm concerned for their safety."

So there it was. She was concerned for their safety. Now, there's nothing wrong with being concerned about your children's well-being, but it had been his experience that along with 'concern' came 'restrictions!' "And...?" he asked.

"And," she replied, "I want Andy and Matt to stay away from those woods for a while."

Robert sat listening and she continued, "You say that old bum hasn't hurt anybody, well how do you know that to be true? The fact is, we don't know anything about him and besides, you've heard the rumors."

"Right, right. The rumors. Let's see. They say he's an escaped convict, right? And what else, oh yeah, they say he was in prison for murder, and the victims were a couple of young boys."

"That's right." Linda said with a slight grin feeling she'd finally got him to see things her way.

"Let me ask you something," he said. "Who is 'they'?"

Linda was puzzled by this question. "I don't understand. What do you mean?"

"'They'. You know, the people who say things about the man in the woods without ever having spoken to him. 'They'."

Okay, there was the stare, the crossed arms and now there was the shaking of the head as if saying, Boy, are you in big trouble.

He continued with his sensible thinking and said,

"Another thing, if 'they' ... don't even know his name or where he comes from, then how do they know so much about his criminal history?"

Robert took a bite of his sandwich and as he chewed he pondered his own questions. "Strange," he mumbled with a mouth full of food.

Linda was furious. Her husband, with his clear headed way of thinking, drove her crazy sometimes. Then something occurred to her. She blurted out, "His name is Pete."

Linda was sure she'd scored a hit with this bit of unknown information and she was feeling good about herself until Robert said, "Does he have a last name, or is that it? Oh, I get it, he's like one of them movie stars who was only one name, like Shane or Ringo. Pete."

"That's his name." she said sternly. "I have overheard the boys talking about him when they thought I wasn't listening. Now, I forbid those boys from going near the woods or that man again, until we learn more about him."

His wife was fuming and he didn't like seeing her this way. He didn't know the boys had actually had contact with the man in the woods. Maybe she was right, he thought.

They really didn't know anything about the man, be it good or bad. And maybe it was best to keep them away from the woods for the time being.

He relented, "Okay Honey, I'll talk to them, but I know they're not gonna be too happy about it."

Linda smiled, clapped her hands together and leaned over to kiss him on his forehead, "Thank you, Honey. I feel much better. Oh, and don't let the boys know this was my idea, I wouldn't want them mad at me."

"Of course honey, I'll take the heat for you, again. Now, can I eat my lunch in peace?"

"Certainly dear, let me freshen your tea for you." She hurried off to the kitchen happily.

Robert thought to himself, why was it he always got the

raw end of the deal? He looked down at his lunch and remembered why he allowed it. He was well taken care of around the Lockhart home and it was a trade-off.

Some folks called it love.

Illustration 11: Sheriff Bryson

CHAPTER 18

Pete was sitting on the floor of the boy's treehouse, the door open and his legs hanging outside. He stared out over the open field looking for them. For a week now they hadn't shown and he wondered what could have happened. Had Ben's condition taken a turn for the worse? Maybe they'd gone on a vacation with the family. Surely they would have told him something. Could be anything, but one thing was for sure, he'd gotten used to the boy's company, and right then he was feeling about as lonely as he had in a while.

Not since the train wreck had he felt this way. Oh sure, the pain and sadness that had consumed him after the wreck was unbearable and there were times when he thought he could not carry on. And this pain was no comparison to that.

It hurt nonetheless. The boy's company helped fill a void, something Pete had missed from his own children. And now, the boys were gone too, and he wasn't sure he'd ever see them again. At least, that was his gut feeling.

He sat there until the sun went down and at last decided he needed to find out what was going on with the boys. And of course, he needed someone to talk to.

Pete closed up the treehouse, climbed to the ground and made his way down the dark pathway. He needed no light, having traveled the trail many times. He would visit with Sheriff Bryson to see what he knew about the boys. Maybe the Sheriff would have a cup of coffee or two for an old friend.

Sheriff Bryson was sitting at his desk going through some complaints that had been filed. Most were minor complaints and some even made him smile. The complaints pretty much told the story of Carbon Hollow. And that story was, there wasn't much going on.

Gary Johnson had sold an old set of retread tires to Billy Ray Johnson, (no relation at least as far as anybody knew), and was still owed three dollars.

Gary claimed that it wasn't so much about the money as it was about principle. Billy Ray should be put in jail to teach him a lesson.

Billy Ray claimed that he'd paid for the tires in full … well, for what they were worth anyway.

The Sheriff thought about the complaint. If he arrested Billy Ray, it would cost the city more than three dollars just to feed him. Then he thought about just paying the three dollars out of his own pocket, but knew that wouldn't work, Gary being so high on principal and all.

He closed the folder and placed the complaint in a file cabinet behind his desk labeled, "No Attention Needed," and hoped the issue would resolve itself. Most complaints in that drawer did.

Next up was a complaint filed by Caroline Baker. According to her, a neighbor's dog comes from two blocks over just to "Do his doody" on her front lawn. The sheriff chuckled at Mrs. Baker's description of the "*offense.*"

The dog is quite large, she goes on to explain, as is the doody the animal deposits on her lawn. Chuckle.

For some unexplained reason the dog simply refuses to do his doody in any other yard but hers. *Chuckle.*

She is requesting that the owner of the dog be ordered

to fence it up, or chain it up and come remove the doody from her lawn. "Chuckle, chuckle".

The Sheriff placed the folder in a drawer labeled "Attention required" and made a mental note to go out and visit the owner of the dog. He smiled and chuckled some more. "Do his doody," he said to himself and shook his head.

He heard a light knock on the rear door of the jail and immediately knew who it was. For years Pete had been visiting him around the first of the month. He took a glance at his wall calendar on his way to let Pete in. A little early, he thought.

The Sheriff killed the lights before he opened the door and after Pete stepped inside, he closed the door and turned them back on.

He turned to Pete and said, "Hey Buddy, how ya doing? A little early ain't you?"

"A little bit. I needed to talk to you. Are you busy?"

The Sheriff looked at his friend with some concern and said, "Naw, not at all. Just doin' some paperwork. Come on in, I'll make us a fresh pot."

Pete followed the Sheriff into his office, and as he busied himself making coffee Pete pulled his old tattered coat off and found a place to sit down.

The Sheriff washed out the coffee pot, put in fresh grounds and water, and placed it on the burner. Then he sat behind the desk and said, "Pete, you okay? You look like you got something on your mind."

"Actually I do, but first I need to tell you something."

Pete then relayed to the Sheriff how he'd befriended Andy, Matt, and Ben. He explained how he'd come to know them, and even about the Ghost Train and how they all heard it.

The Sheriff sat without saying a word. He was entranced by the story, especially by the Ghost Train.

Pete waited for the Sheriff to pour them coffee and after slowly taking a sip he continued, "Anyway Charlie, I ain't seen the boys in a week and I'm a little worried. Especially for Ben. I understand he's not well."

The Sheriff didn't say anything right away. He was deep in thought. He and Pete had been friends since they were kids, and he knew the real story of why Pete lived in the woods. Countless times the Sheriff had offered to help him, begged him in fact ... but Pete had always declined any help.

Hearing that Pete had befriended the boys was encouraging. It was progress. As far as he knew Pete had not spoken to or had contact with anyone but him for years.

Maybe his old friend was starting to come around, he thought. And the news he was about to tell him wouldn't help. He thought about not saying anything, but knew he'd find out eventually.

With a stiff lip the Sheriff said, "Ben's in the hospital, Pete. Doc says the prognosis ain't good. The only hope is a donor."

Pete was stunned and sat without speaking, the coffee getting cold in his hand.

The Sheriff added, "That might explain why they ain't been out to see you."

"But you said Ben just went to the hospital last night. I ain't seen any one of them for a week."

The Sheriff shrugged and said, "Ben's been confined to his house for over a week now. Andy and Matt's probably just been stayin' close. You understand?"

It made sense Pete thought, but he wasn't convinced. He was sure they were close enough friends that one of the boys would have gotten word to him about Ben.

"How long?" Pete asked.

"How long for what?" The Sheriff asked, not understanding at first, but then realizing what Pete wanted to know. "Ah, how long?"

Both men held each other's gaze for what seemed an eternity. Finally the Sheriff said, "Doc Martin says maybe these days, a week at the most."

Pete's eyes closed and his head drooped until his chin was resting on his chest. The air seemed to have left his body.

Sheriff Bryson stood, walked over to his friend and placed a hand on Pete's shoulder, "Are you okay? Let me get you some water."

The Sheriff went to the bathroom sink to get the water, but when he returned Pete was gone. He moved quickly to the back door and looked outside. Pete was nowhere in sight. He thought about running after Pete, but knew it would be useless. There was no way he'd find him in the dark. Pete befriending the boys had been a good sign, and the Sheriff had hoped that his old friend might finally recover. But obviously the news about Ben had devastated him. The Sheriff locked up his office for the night and slipped behind the wheel of his cruiser. As he drove home he replayed the night's events and the talk that they had had, and decided he would go out at first light to talk to Pete. Pete needed a friend now more than ever, and that was the least he could do. After all, Pete had saved the Sheriff's life.

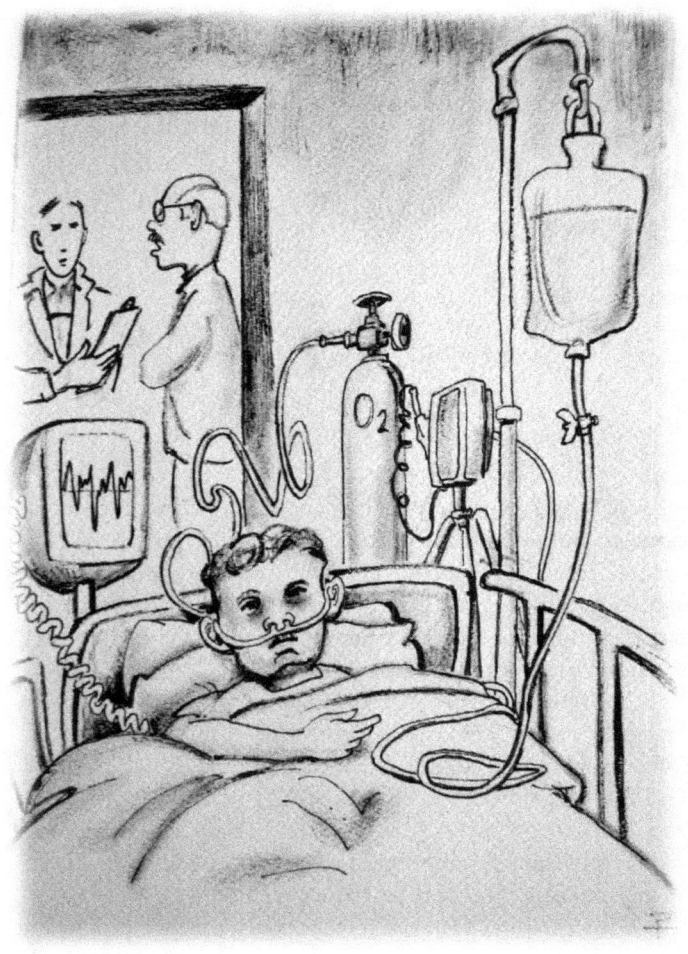

Illustration 12: Ben in the Hospital

CHAPTER 19

I was working at the grocery store when my father came rushing down the aisle and I saw the frightened look on his face. Right away, I knew something terrible had happened. It was the middle of the afternoon and my father should be at work, but he wasn't. "Andy, its Ben. We need to get to the hospital now."

I didn't hesitate. I didn't tell anyone I was leaving. I just dropped what I was doing and followed my father outside to his truck.

Matt was waiting in the cab with a worried look on his face. Dad drove faster than he ever had and we made it to the hospital in less than ten minutes. Neither of us spoke during the ride. We were too afraid to.

At the hospital Dad parked the truck and we practically ran to the entrance of the emergency room. Once inside we saw Mom talking to a nurse and she motioned us over when she saw us.

Mom hugged us and said, "He's in the O.R., no one is allowed in except immediate family."

"Any word on his condition?" My father asked.

Mom shrugged, and with tears in her eyes she said, "He collapsed while watching TV. Other than that, I don't know anything. We'll just have to wait." Dad nodded and led us towards the crowded waiting room. Apparently word had spread, and there were several people there in support of Ben and his parents.

Mom and Dad had wandered over to where the grown-ups were gathered, speaking in soft, hushed voices. Matt and I found a place to stand away from the crowd. We looked each other in the eye and knew what the other was thinking, our friend was out of time.

We were heartbroken and teary-eyed. Never had we felt such grief. It was unbearable.

An hour later Ben's father walked through the double doors that led to the O.R. and hung his head. He stood there oblivious to the rest of us.

My father spoke first, "Walter."

Mr. Gordon walked towards us, dragging his feet as if he didn't have the strength to lift them. The color was gone from his face, and he appeared to be only half alive.

He said, his voice trembling, "He's stable."

Though some of the adults breathed a sigh of relief, we knew there was more.

My father asked, "But...?" his question summed up in a word what we were all wondering.

Mr. Gordon broke down and started crying. He was barely intelligible. "This is it Robert, my boy's almost gone."

My father had to catch Mr. Gordon from dropping to the floor. He was sobbing uncontrollably and dad helped him to a nearby bench.

When Mr. Gordon was calm enough to talk, he filled us in on what Doc Martin had determined. "The Doc's got him stable, but *sob* he says *sob* Ben's got maybe *sob* forty-eight hours."

At that point, Mr. Gordon had lost all control and a nurse had to bring a wheelchair to retrieve him. She explained that Mrs. Gordon had already been given a sedative and was relaxing in Ben's room. She'd see to it that Mr. Gordon was taken care of as well.

The mood in the waiting room was as bad as it gets. Not a dry eye in the room. The news had devastated us all.

Matt, who'd been standing at my side the whole time tugged my shirt and motioned with his head for me to follow him. He led the way until we found the men's restroom, and once inside, we checked the stalls to make sure we were alone. We were.

Matt blurted out, "We got to tell Pete."

"Why, what's he gonna do? Besides, I don't want to leave the hospital in case something happens to Ben. I want to be close by."

Now Matt was crying. "Please Andy. Pete can save him. You know he can. We've got to talk to him Andy. Please."

I couldn't bear to see my little brother so desperate and heartbroken. I put my arm around his shoulders. "Okay, I'll go find him, but you stay here and cover for me."

Matt whimpered, "Talk to him, Andy. Make him see he's Ben's only chance."

"I will Matt, I promise. Now, you go back to the waiting room with the others."

Matt headed in one direction and I went in the other. Just as I was about to step outside of the hospital, Mr. and Mrs. Taylor came walking through the door, Maryanne right behind them.

I stopped dead in my tracks and Mr. Taylor said, "Oh Andy, we heard what happened. I closed up the store and we got here as fast as we could. How's Ben?"

"Stable, Mr. Taylor. Everyone's in the waiting room," I said pointing in the direction of the crowd.

"And how about you and Matt, how're you boys holding up?"

What could I say? I wanted to break down and cry. I wanted to scream. But deep inside me still felt like Ben had a chance. "I ain't gonna lie Mr. Taylor, it ain't easy. But I'm not giving up on Ben just yet."

Mr. and Mrs. Traylor smiled and nodded, then headed towards the crowd. Maryanne lingered behind and after her parents were out of earshot she said, "Andy, are you okay? Where are you going?"

I suddenly remembered where I was heading and said, "I'm sorry Maryanne, I need to go. I'll talk to you when I get back."

I didn't stop running until I got to Taylor's Grocery, where I found that my bike was locked inside.

I had no choice but to look for Pete on foot. I ran all the way to the treehouse, when I got there I could barely breathe.

It took some doing, but finally I caught my breath and started calling for Pete. I shouted, "Pete! Pete! I need to talk to you! It's Ben! He's in the hospital! Pete, can you hear me?"

I waited, but there was no response. "Peeeete! We need you! Please help us!"

I thought about searching the woods for Pete's cave, but knew that would take too much time. Then a thought occurred to me, I would leave him a note.

After searching every pocket and not finding anything to leave a note with, I got an idea. From the campfire I found a piece of charcoaled wood, grabbed it and climbed the ladder to the treehouse.

I was about to write a note on the treehouse door, but stopped. I thought long and hard about what to say. How could I possibly ask Pete to do something like that? I had no right.

Ben's heart condition had always been there. It had nothing to do with the Ghost Train or Pete. I decided I would leave a short note to let Pete know about Ben. After all, Pete was our friend.

I scribbled the message on the treehouse door the best I could and hoped Pete would see it and come check on Ben. There was really nothing else to do, so I tried calling for Pete one last time and after getting no response, I climbed to the ground and ran back towards town.

* * * * *

Pete had been standing back in the shadows of the trees when Andy came running up. He could see him and hear him calling clearly, but something caused him to stay put.

Why did he not want to talk to the boy? He asked himself. But, he already knew the answer. Andy would ask difficult questions, and he would not have the answers the boy wanted to hear.

He watched as Andy climbed the ladder to the treehouse and appeared to be scribbling something on the door, but he was too far away to make out the writing. He was sure the boy was leaving him a message, but he decided not to interrupt. He'd read if after the boy had gone.

Andy called out to him one more time, and he could almost hear the desperation in the boy's voice.

When he was sure Andy was far away, Pete walked quietly through the woods until he was standing at the base of the tree that held the treehouse. He looked up and saw the message Andy had marked on the treehouse door, and as he read it, his heart tightened.

Ben - Hospital
48 hours - Tops

Pete felt all the energy leave his body as he dropped to his knees. He spoke to himself, "Where are you now, God? Where are you now that another child needs you?"

Then he fell forward face first into the dirt. He sobbed and cursed God some more, until he passed out.

He wasn't sure how long he was out, but when he did come around the sun had already set.

Pete stood on wobbling legs and wiped the dirt from

his clothes and face. His tears, mixed with the dirt, had caused mud to be stuck to his face. He barely noticed it. He needed to see the Sheriff and there was no time to waste.

CHAPTER 20

Sheriff Bryson had been so absorbed in thought that he barely heard the knock on the rear door of the jail. In fact, he wasn't even sure he *had* heard a knock, until he heard it again. He moved quickly to the door, and when he opened it, he found Pete standing there covered in dirt and looking ten, maybe twenty years older than he had just a few days before.

The Sheriff said, "Pete, I almost didn't hear you knock. Come on in. Man, you look kinda rough. What's happened to you?"

Pete made an attempt at light humor, but he didn't pull it off. "You mean rougher than normal?"

"Come on, I'll make us some coffee. Have a seat."

Pete declined both and said, "I heard about the boy."

The Sheriff only nodded and waited for Pete to say what was on his mind.

"Charlie, I need you to check on something for me. And I'd like you to keep it just between us."

"Sure," the Sheriff said, curious about the way his friend was behaving, "What can I do for you?"

Pete made his request and the Sheriff just stood there with a puzzled look on his face. For the life of him, Sheriff

98

Bryson couldn't understand why Pete would be needing *that* kind of information, but he was about to find out.

"Now, why in the world would you need to know something like that? What are you planning to do? I want to know or I won't help."

"Fine, don't help then," Pete said and turned to walk out.

The Sheriff said, "Wait. Just wait. Of course I'll get the information for you. I'm just worried for you, that's all."

Pete stood there not saying a word and finally the Sheriff asked, "Okay, how soon do you need it?"

"Right now," Pete replied bluntly.

"Now! Come on, I don't know if I can get it right away. Can't it wait until the morning?"

Pete just stared.

"Okay, give me a minute while I make some phone calls."

While the Sheriff was on the phone, Pete found some writing paper, a pen and an envelope. He quickly jotted something on the paper, then placed it in the envelope and sealed it.

The Sheriff hung up the phone and handed Pete a piece of paper with the information he'd requested scribbled on it.

Pete felt sure what the information would reveal, but when he saw it in writing he just hung his head and nodded as if coming to some conclusion in his mind. The note confirmed what he already knew.

Sheriff Bryson said, "Now, are you gonna tell me what's going on or not?"

Pete handed the envelope he'd been holding in his hand to the Sheriff and said, "If anything should ever happen to me, I want you to open this *immediately* and follow the instructions. Do you understand?"

"Well, no, I don't understand Pete. You ain't making no kinda sense."

Pete stepped close to his friend with their faces only

inches apart, "Do you understand? Immediately!"

The Sheriff sighed and nodded, "I understand. You can count on me."

Pete raised his hand for the Sheriff to take and when he did the Sheriff was surprised at how firm and strong the handshake was.

Pete said, "Goodbye, old friend."

The Sheriff was surprised by Pete's comments, they left him speechless.

Pete pulled his hand from the Sheriff's grip, turned, and walked out the door.

Bryson just stood there, staring at the door as it closed. He looked at the envelope in his hand and suddenly realized what it all meant. He said in a soft voice even though his friend was already gone, "Goodbye, Pete."

CHAPTER 21

It was late, and though some of the visitors in the waiting room had gone home for the evening, there were still quite a few there. Matt and I sat on a sofa with Maryanne and Andrea. The crowd was quite subdued and when anyone spoke it was in a whisper. Everyone's thoughts and prayers were the same – Ben needed a donor, and soon.

It seemed an impossibility that one would come through with so little time left. Ben had been waiting for a couple of years, and it didn't seem likely one would come in a matter of hours. Still, we all clung to hope.

I saw Mom whisper something to Dad and when he nodded she stood and walked towards us. "Come along, boys. I think it's best if we went home. You two need some rest."

Matt said, "I don't want to go home, Mom. What if Ben needs us?"

Mom had a sad look on her face and with a soft voice she said, "Matt honey, the only thing we can do for Ben is pray. Now let's go home so you boys can get some sleep. We'll come back first thing in the morning. Besides, your father will be here, and he'll let us know right away if there's a change."

We said goodbye to Maryanne and Andrea and followed Mom out of the hospital. Neither of us spoke on the short ride home though Mom had tried to comfort us.

We were drained emotionally and went straight to our room, put on pajamas and climbed into bed. Matt asked me, "Did you find Pete?"

All I could do was shake my head. I was too exhausted to get into that discussion. No sooner had my head hit the pillow than I was asleep.

I came wide awake at around three in the morning, though it felt I had only slept ten minutes or so. I lay there listening for the sound that had awakened me. Then I heard it again. It was the sound of a train whistle.

At first it seemed far away, but it got louder and closer. And just like before, what I thought was a whistle was actually people screaming. Dead people.

I managed to turn and look at Matt. He too was awake, staring at the ceiling, listening. Then it was gone as quickly as it had come.

We lay there crying in the darkness of our bedroom knowing what had just happened. The Ghost Train had taken Ben.

Matt fell back asleep before I did. I was lost in thought. I thought about Pete, and asked myself a couple of "What-ifs?"

I also wondered if Pete had heard the train. Then I drifted off to sleep again.

* * * * *

Our father came rushing into our bedroom at a little after six in the morning, and there was urgency in his voice. "Get up, boys, we've got to get to the hospital. Something's happened."

I tried to wipe the sleep from my puffy eyes, and said, "He's gone Dad, that's what happened. We heard it."

Dad gave me a puzzled look. "What are you talkin' about? What did you hear?"

Matt half-shouted at our dad. "The train, Dad, we heard the Ghost Train, and now Ben's gone. Can't you see?"

"I have no idea what you two are babbling on about, but it'll have to wait until later. Right now, we have to get to the hospital A.S.A.P. Now get dressed, I'll be waiting in the truck."

We dressed slowly, not looking forward to the scene at the hospital. We knew how difficult that was going to be. When dad blew the horn we stepped it up a bit, and a few minutes later we were on the way to the hospital. We'd decided to sit in the truck's bed, not wanting to ride in the cab with our father in case he wanted to talk.

We had inadvertently blurted out about the Ghost Train in a sleep haze, and knew there would be questions later. Up until then, we had never breathed a word about the train to anyone. Well, except Pete.

We hurried into the hospital waiting room and immediately saw the change in the mood of the visitors. The night before it had been somber, with a feeling of lost hope. There had been silent prayers, hand holding, and whispers. But that had all changed. There was still a lot of crying, but Matt and I stopped dead in our tracks when we saw the mood of the crowd before us.

The tears flowing were tears of joy and the mood was ... well ... jubilant, to say the least.

We stood there with our mouths wide open and in shock. Dad, who'd gone ahead to see what had happened, came rushing back to us and said excitedly. "Oh my God. It's a miracle. You're not going to believe this!"

"What, Dad? What's happened?" Matt shouted.

"Ben's alive, son. A donor came in last night. He's going to be okay."

We started crying as our father gripped us in a bear hug and held us for what seemed like an eternity. The strain of the events of the past few weeks had drained us completely.

I pulled away from dad and said, "Can we see him now?"

Dad shook his head and said, "He's in a hospital in Cincinnati. He was flown there early this morning. But I was told the surgery went well."

Matt and I were grinning from ear to ear though our eyes were puffy and wet. Matt asked, "Dad, can we go to Cincinnati?"

Dad appeared to be in thought, then said, "Tell you what... let me see how long Ben's gonna be there, and if he can accept visitors. If we're allowed to visit, we'll go up to Cincinnati in a day or so."

Dad tousled our hair and said, "Why don't you boys go find your mother. I think she's here somewhere. Maybe she'll buy you some breakfast. I'm gonna go see what else I can find out."

After dad walked away, I turned to Matt and smiled. Words could not describe what we were feeling.

Ben had not gotten a ride on the Ghost Train. It looked like old Pete was right after all. I said to Matt, "We've got to find Pete and tell him what's happened. You want to go with me?"

"Sure Andy, but can we get something to eat first? I'm starved."

"Sounds good. We'll go later, after things calm down," I replied.

I put my arm around my brother's shoulder and we headed out in search of our mother.

*   *   *   *   *

Later that afternoon Matt and I were pushing our bikes from the garage and was just about to jump on them when our father called down to us from the front porch. He was sipping iced tea and he said, "Where you boys headin'?"

"Uh, we wuz goin' to tell all of Ben's friends the good news," I lied.

Dad didn't believe us for a second. He knew full well where we were going, but I guess he decided to cut us some slack under the circumstances.

"Okay fellas, but y'all be back by supper time. You wouldn't want to get on your Mom's bad side."

We shoved off down the drive and called back over our shoulders at Dad, "We'll be here, thanks."

Dad smiled at us and shouted back, "Say hello to Pete for me."

We looked back at Dad and waved. It surprised us that he could see right through our plan. But not really, after all, he was a grown-up, and grown-ups had special powers.

CHAPTER 22

Matt caught up with me and said, "How do you think Dad knew we wuz goin' to see old Pete?"

"It's one of those grown-up things," I said. "They just know stuff, like how to read kid's minds. Kinda scary when you think about it."

"Creepy is more like it. If they knew some of the stuff I think about, they'd ground me for life." Matt said.

"Don't worry so much. They can only read your thoughts when you look them in the eye. From now on, try not to make eye contact with them if you're thinking stuff you don't want them to know about."

Matt asked, "How am I supposed to do that when Mom always says, 'Look at me when I'm talking to you'?"

"Its simple dummy, when that happens just pretend you have a bellyache and Mom will forget about what you two were talking about. She'll be all worried about you and her maternal instincts will kick in. All she'll want to do is take care of you."

"I don't know about that idea, Andy. Mom will just try to give me some Castor Oil. I think I'd rather her know what I was thinking than take that stuff."

I rolled my eyes at Matt and said, "Boy, you've got

problems." Then I kicked it in and pedaled as fast as I could. I wanted to put some distance between me and Matt and his stupid questions.

Matt was a little out of breath from trying to keep up with me, but he asked, "Do you know where Pete's cave is?"

"No, but I got a pretty good idea. I'm betting it's close to that fishing hole he takes us to."

"How do you know that?"

I gave him my reasoning, "I don't, for sure, it's just a hunch. But think about it, Pete always acts kinda funny when he takes us there. I'm thinkin' he's afraid we'll find his cave."

I continued, "Matt, you know how secretive we are about our treehouse? Well, he's probably the same way about his cave. He just don't want nobody to find it."

Matt said, "Well, that makes sense, I guess."

"Come on, Squirt, we're burning daylight." We headed down a trail and into the woods.

When we made it to the fishing hole, I said to Matt, "Okay, here's what we're gonna do. You go that way about fifty paces then turn left and make a circle around the pond. I'll do the same in the other direction."

I could see Matt was worried about being left alone in the woods, so I said, "Listen, just keep your eye on the pond. Never let it out of your sight. We can always meet back there."

He said, "What do I do if I find the cave?"

I thought then said, "You got your whistle with you?"

Matt dug around in his pants pocket and fished out a handful of items. He had a ball of string, a yo-yo, a couple of rubber bands, a Band-Aid and most important, a whistle he'd gotten from a box of Cracker Jacks.

He held it up and said, "Got it."

"Good, now head out and if you find Pete's cave, just blow the whistle and keep blowing until I find you."

We headed off in opposite directions and when I

looked behind me I saw that Matt had the whistle held tightly between his lips. Also, he was paying more attention to the pond then looking for Pete's cave.

Barely ten minutes into the search, I spotted it, or what I thought might be Pete's cave. There were a lot of dead tree branches and shrubs piled up in an area I thought might be an opening of the cave.

I shouted to Matt and kept shouting until he came rushing through the woods toward my voice. When he walked up I smiled and said, "I found it."

Illustration 13: Army Foot Locker Holds

All the Secrets of Hobo Pete

CHAPTER 23

We quickly removed the branches and shrubs then stood back staring at the dark opening of the cave.

Matt shouted into the cave, "Pete! Are you in there?" He voice echoed into the darkness.

I smacked him on the shoulder and said, "He ain't in there, stupid. If he was, these branches wouldn't be stacked up on the opening."

Matt thought a second then said, "What if he was able to pull them over the opening from inside? Maybe he did it to keep us from finding him. Or maybe to keep bears out."

Some of the stuff Matt was saying made sense, but I doubted Pete was in there. After all, it was the middle of the afternoon. Still, I was curious and wanted to see the inside.

I motioned for Matt to follow me into the cave and he said, "Maybe we should come back later?"

I could see his reluctance and said, "Stop acting like a girl, Jeeez."

Hanging from a belt loop on my jeans was a pen-light keychain. I grabbed it and turned it on as we inched into the cave. The pen-light wasn't very bright, but it was better than nothing.

Matt clung to my shirttail, but I made no attempt to pushing him away. To be honest, I was scared myself.

The cave smelled of musty dirt and damp, soot-covered walls. Pete must have had a campfire in there somewhere, I thought.

The deeper we got into the cave, the cooler it got. We'd been on a steady decline for about the last hundred feet or so. I was about to give up and leave when my pen-light flashed onto something on the floor.

We inched closer and Matt said, "What's that?"

Our eyes had adjusted some and the light was bright enough for us to see a pile of old blankets stacked near the wall. Then we saw a burned-out campfire, and several rusted pots and pans.

"It's Pete's camp. This must be where he lives."

There was a lot of odds and ends scattered about and I couldn't help but think, other peoples' trash. But Pete apparently had use for it.

There were bottles and cans and even an old broken wooden lawn chair. I guessed Pete probably used it as firewood.

I scanned the area with my pen-light and was surprised when it shown on a box sitting behind the pile of blankets.

The box was maybe three feet long and two feet wide. It was painted green though the color was almost faded. Stenciled on the top was the letters, 'U.S. Army'.

"What is that Andy?"

"It looks like an old army foot locker. Grandpa had one like it. I saw it in his attic once."

I reached down and flipped the latch. There wasn't a lock on it so I opened it. When we saw what was inside, I whistled in astonishment.

The locker was full. Full of things that appealed to young boys. There were several items of military memorabilia such as medals and ribbons. There was even a uniform and a green helmet. What was even more surprising was that everything was clean. I mean the medals even sparkled when the light hit them.

"Wow," Matt exclaimed, "look at all this cool stuff. Do you think it belongs to Pete, or do you think he stole it?"

An old faded envelope caught my eye and I reached for it. I gently opened the delicate envelope and removed its contents.

Inside there was some official looking documents and I scanned them quickly without reading everything that was typed onto the pages.

Three lines in particular caught my eye.

"United States Army," "Captain Peter Hanson" and "Honorable Discharge."

"It's Pete's," I said, then held the documents out for Matt to see. "Pete was in the Army and he was a Captain, no less."

"Holy Cow, a Captain! Old Hobo Pete. It's hard to imagine." Matt said, amazed at the discovery. He reached into the box and pulled out an old tattered photo album. "Hey, check this out."

I took the album from Matt and noticed how delicate and fragile it was. Obviously Pete had owned it for some time.

Slowly, I opened it and found that it was filled with old black and white photos. Some were of Pete either standing alone or with men I didn't recognize. But most were of him with a woman and two young children. "This must be Pete's family." I showed the photo to Matt.

As I flipped to the next page an old brown and fading newspaper clipping fell to the floor. I retrieved it from the floor and held the light close to it.

There was a photo of a train wreck. Passenger cars were strewn about, lying on their sides. There were a lot of people standing around but most looked to be either law enforcement or medical officials. The headline read:

"Worst Train Wreck in U.S. History"

177 Dead - 1 Missing

I whistled as I read the article to Matt. Apparently there was a set of railroad tracks that passed through Carbon Hollow. But that was a decade ago. It seemed there was a dangerous curve along the line and there had even been a couple of mishaps.

Then, one night a southbound passenger train hit the curve at too high a rate of speed and it derailed. Of the 177 passengers on board, all were killed accept one, and it was presumed that passenger was killed as well.

After that, the tracks were removed and never again would a train pass through Carbon Hollow, the article claimed.

Matt asked what we were both thinking, "Andy, do you think Pete was the passenger that was missing?"

Before I could answer there was a blinding light shined in our eyes and a deep voice said, "It's him."

CHAPTER 24

Sheriff Bryson lowered his flashlight and said, "Pete was on that train that night and he was the only survivor. But now he's gone."

The Sheriff had frightened us and I said as much, "Holy crap Sheriff, you scared the bejeezus out of us! We didn't even hear you walk up."

"What are you boys doin' in here?" he said.

Matt quickly said, "We wuz looking for Pete. We wanted to tell him the good news about Ben." Matt had another thought, "We didn't bother anything Sheriff, we wuz just lookin'. Are you gonna arrest us?"

Sheriff Bryson looked sadly at the boys and thought, *"So, they don't know yet."*

I asked, "Sheriff, what did you mean when you said, he's gone? Where'd Pete go?"

The Sheriff didn't say anything until he'd gathered some kindling and started a fire. He sat down on the pile of blankets and Matt and I sat next to each other on the footlocker.

Sheriff Bryson began to tell us the story of Hobo Pete.

He stoked the fire with a stick and said, "His name was Peter Hanson. And he was my friend."

"Pete and I were raised together, and when we were young, we were like two crossed fingers," the Sheriff said, holding up his hand and crossing a couple of fingers. To further indicate just how close they were, he said, "Where you saw one of us, the other was close by. We learned to hunt together right here in these same woods." That explained why Pete knew his way around, I thought. "We went to school together, and played football on the same team. The first car we bought, we split the cost and taught ourselves how to drive, though it dang near killed us. When we graduated high school, the Japs had just bombed Pearl Harbor only a few months before, so we both marched down to the recruiting office and joined the Army. For four long years we fought them Japs in the South Pacific. God what a living hell that was. Still can't believe we made it out alive. We were in the infantry, and Pete was made for the stuff. During the war, he saved my life. He took a bullet in his chest, and had he not, I wouldn't be here today. He had a heck of a time surviving that gunshot, but he did, and never once did he complain or hold it over my head. I wasn't the only one Pete saved during the war. He saved countless lives with his bravery. That's what all those medals were for that you found in his box."

The Sheriff hung his head, and had a sad look on his face. He appeared to have lost his train of thought. But then he continued.

"Pete and I made it home alive though, like I was saying. And both of us with honorable discharges. I was a Staff Sergeant and Pete was a Captain."

He had a smile on his face as he said, "I'll tell you, the girls just loved us in our uniforms. But we weren't boys anymore. We were men. Men who'd grown up too fast and had killed, and had seen too much death to ever be young again. That's what war does to you. It kills you and ages you. Either way, you ain't never the same. Pete was a real American hero boys and don't forget it. The people in this town have a habit of that. Forgettin'."

Again he hung his head, and we thought he must be drifting back in time and remembering things. "This town never knew Pete like I did. He wasn't one to blow his own horn, so the town folk never knew about his heroics during the war. In fact, shortly after we returned from the war they'd forgotten that Pete and I had ever been in the military. They just went on with their lives. I ran for Sheriff not long after coming home, and actually won. The old Sheriff was retiring and I really didn't have anybody running against me. I've been Sheriff ever since."

"My first order of business as Sheriff was to appoint a deputy. And I had just the right fella in mind. But Pete wasn't interested and told me he'd decided he was gonna move up north and go to work for one of the big auto makers up there. And that's just what he did. He spent several years up there and I'd get a letter or postcard from him now and then. A couple of times he sent some photographs of him and a woman he'd married. Then they had kids, a boy and a girl, and he'd send photos of them as well. One day, I received a letter from Pete and he explained that he and his family were moving to Carbon Hollow, and he wanted to know if the deputy job was still open. I was excited to say the least. I was looking forward to seeing my old friend. He and his family would be arriving by train and I was supposed to meet them at the train depot."

"Well, the train didn't stop in Carbon Hollow and the closest stop was over in Martinsville about twenty miles from here. I was there waiting on them when I got the news. The train had derailed and killed everyone on board, save for one person. I learned later that the one missing was Pete. It took the rail company six months to find all the bodies and clean the mess up. When the clean-up was over the rail company sent me a letter out of courtesy to the Sheriff's Department, they said, since the information was confidential. All the note said was, Peter Hanson. Time went by, and months after the train wreck, I was sitting in my office going over paperwork when I heard a light knock on the rear door of the jail. When

I went to go see who it was, there stood Pete. He was such a mess, I barely recognized him. Pete had long hair and a beard that was dirty, and the clothes he was wearing were torn and tattered. I invited him in and we sat for a couple of hours drinking coffee and I was even able to round him up something to eat. It was obvious that train wreck and the loss of his family had changed him. Try as I may, he would not accept my offer to help him get cleaned up and get himself together. He told me he'd been living in this old cave here since the wreck, because it was close to the last place his family was alive."

The Sheriff explained that the crash site was close by, although the tracks had been taken up years before.

He continued, "Anyway, that's how it's been for the past few years. Pete shows up at my office about once a month. We sit, play checkers, and drink coffee. Not much else, though. The town people don't even recognize Pete. They don't remember him being one of us. And they ain't put two and two together yet, and figured out that Pete was the one never found in the train wreck. They're always wanting me to arrest him or run him out of town. I've wanted to tell them who he was, but Pete wouldn't let me. So I respected his wishes."

The story Sheriff Bryson was telling Matt and I had us hanging on every word and sitting on the edge of our seat. Pete was a real life hero. He wasn't no murderer like everyone claimed. He had lost his family and now we understood him so much more than before.

Matt spoke up, "Sheriff, you said Pete was gone. Where'd he go?"

Sheriff Bryson had tears in his eyes as he hung his head. I instinctively knew the Sheriff was about to give us some bad news. You could see it in his face. And when he did, it was in the same slow manner in which he'd told us the story of our friend Pete.

He said, "Pete came by the jail last night, and he was acting kinda strange. He would not have coffee with me or sit and talk. He just wanted information. When he first asked me for it, I tried to find out what he wanted it for, but he wouldn't tell me. He was very insistent that I get it for him though. I made a phone call and got the information he'd requested. I'd written it down on some notebook paper and when I passed it to him, and after he read it, he pulled an envelope out of his pocket and handed it to me. Then he said the strangest thing. He told me that if anything should ever happen to him, I was supposed to open the envelope *immediately*. He was very adamant about that and of course, I promised him I would. At the time, I didn't put it all together, but its all clear now. After I promised to do as he asked, Pete shook my hand and said, "Goodbye, Charlie," then turned and walked out of the back door of the jail. Now, the unusual part about that was the fact that we almost never shook hands. I mean, we have in the past, but not like that. This handshake seemed so ... final. I started to go after him but he'd disappeared too quickly. I decided to look for him this morning but never got the chance."

Matt asked, "What was the information he wanted, Sheriff? What did you find for him?"

Sheriff Bryson looked at us for the longest time, his face shining with sweat and flickering in the fire light. We were holding our breath knowing the information would be something big - something important.

Finally the Sheriff said, "He wanted to know what Ben's blood type was."

We were confused, and didn't understand why Pete would need that kind of information. It made no sense to us.

The Sheriff saw our confusion and explained. "Boys, you can't donate your heart to someone unless you and that person have the same blood type. Pete was checking to see if his and Ben's blood type were the same."

I understood then, and the gravity of that realization hit me hard. Matt hadn't caught on yet.

He said, "Why would Pete want to know something like that, Sheriff?"

I elbowed Matt, and with tears in my eyes, I said, "Because, Pete was gonna donate his heart to Ben."

Matt still didn't get it and said, "But wouldn't he die if he..." then it hit him. He understood what had happened.

The sheriff said, "I was home and in bed asleep when I got a call from one of my deputies. He told me that a body had been found outside the hospital and it looked like Pete. The deputy identified him as, "That old Hobo that lives out in the woods." I hung up on the deputy and jumped out of bed. The envelope Pete had given me was laying on the nightstand, so I tore it open, just as Pete had instructed me to do. Pete had scribbled a short note on a piece of paper and there were instructions there telling me what I should do if anything happened to him. As soon as I read the instructions, I called the hospital and found that Doc Martin was there tending to Ben. I read the note to Doc Martin, then hung up, dressed and got to the hospital as quickly as possible."

"What did the note say?" I asked.

Without saying a word, Sheriff Bryson pulled the note from the shirt pocket of his uniform and passed it to me.

I unfolded it and Matt leaned in close as we read the note together. It read:

> Charlie,
> If you're reading this, then I'm already gone. I'm with my family now. Make sure Ben gets my heart.
> Goodbye, old friend.

I raised my head and said to the Sheriff, "Pete saved Ben's life. How did he die?"

The Sheriff replied, "Andy, you boys shouldn't concern yourselves with how Pete died. Just know that Pete was a brave man, and he gave his own life to save your friend. But also know that Pete was in a lot of pain. He missed his family terribly and I believe losing them the way he did was just more than he could *bare*."

We were thinking about what Sheriff Bryson had just said. Matt said, with a heavy sigh, "Pete was our friend too, and I'm gonna miss him. But if he's with his family now, I think that's a good thing."

The three of us sat and stared into the fire, our thoughts wandering. Finally, the Sheriff said, "Come on boys, I'll give y'all a ride home."

He kicked some dirt over the fire and something occurred to me. I said, "Hey Sheriff, what about the footlocker?"

The Sheriff thought for a second then said, "There's some pretty cool stuff in there, huh?"

"There sure is, Sheriff," Matt said, "what are you gonna do with it?"

"Tell you what, why don't you boys hold onto it. I think Pete would have wanted it that way."

"Cool," I said, then to Matt, "help me would you?" We both grabbed a handle and followed Sheriff Bryson to his police cruiser. At the vehicle, he helped us load the locker box into the trunk of his car, then waited on us to retrieve our bikes, which he also placed inside the trunk.

On the ride to our house, the Sheriff flashed the red and blue emergency lights and even sounded the siren a couple of times.

CHAPTER 25

When Sheriff Bryson pulled to the curb in front of our house, Mom and Dad came running out to meet us, concerned that something bad had happened, since we were being brought home in a squad car.

The Sheriff let them know that we were alright and that he was just giving us a ride home. Mom, seeing that all was okay, headed back to the house, but Dad lingered around while we unloaded our bikes and the locker box.

"What's that?" He asked as Matt and I lugged the box towards the garage.

Sheriff Bryson said, "I can explain it."

We watched them from the garage door and the Sheriff and Dad talked for about twenty minutes. We guessed that the Sheriff was telling him about Pete. We guessed correctly.

After the Sheriff left, Dad rushed straight for the house so Matt and I went to the back door and listened through the screen door.

Mom was in the kitchen when Dad said, "Honey, you're not gonna believe this!"

"What is it? What on earth is going on? Are the boys in trouble?"

"No, no, nothing like that. It's about that old bum who lived in the woods. What was his name?"

"Pete." Mom said.

"That's right, Pete. Well it turns out that Pete ... is a bona fide war hero. The Sheriff's known him since they were kids. They were in World War II together, and Pete even saved the Sheriff's life."

Mom was shocked and in disbelief. "Honey, are you sure? So why was he living out in the woods like some old hobo if he was this big hero? Didn't he have family or friends?"

"Yes," Dad said excitedly, "but you remember that train wreck back in fifty-one? Well, Pete was the one passenger they never found. His wife and children were on that train."

Mom had her hands over her mouth now as Dad told her the story. We could see the sadness on her face through the screen door.

Dad said, "The Sheriff says Pete just lost it after that and stayed in the woods so he could be close to his family."

Mom had teared up and was emotional now. "Oh my God. That poor man. He must be in so much pain."

"Well, not anymore. He committed suicide last night out in front of the hospital. The heart that Ben got was his."

Tears were really pouring down Mom's cheeks then, and she said, "How do you know that?"

Dad told Mom about how Pete had asked the Sheriff to find out what Ben's blood type was and about the note he'd left with the Sheriff.

Mom was speechless and Dad said, "Honey, we've got to do something for Pete."

"What are you saying? What do you mean, 'We've got to do something for Pete?'"

"Not we, like me and you. I'm talking about the people of this town. Pete was a war hero and he saved Ben's life. I think we should honor him some way."

"What are you thinking?" Mom asked.

"I'm not sure yet, but I'm gonna call a special emergency meeting of the town council. This town needs to recognize who Pete was. Honey, I gotta go. I may be late for supper."

Mom hugged Dad and said, "Honey, you're such a good man. You go talk to them, and make them listen. I'll save you some supper."

As Dad rushed out of the house, Matt and I smiled at each other. The last two days had certainly been incredible.

Illustration 14: Andy Working at Taylor's Grocery

CHAPTER 26

I was sweeping the sidewalk in front of Taylor's Grocery and though it was barely ten in the morning, I was sweating from the heat. It was going to be another hot one that was for sure. It was the last day of summer recess and school would start up again on Monday. I was looking forward to it. Many of my friends had been off to summer camps or on vacation with their families, and I hadn't seen a lot of them.

Matt and Ben came riding up on their bikes and I noticed a carton of fiddler worms hanging from the handle bars of Matt's bike. There were several cane poles slung across the bars of Ben's bike.

Matt grinned at me and said jokingly, "Hey Andy, that's a nice dress."

I looked down at the white apron I was wearing and said, "It's an apron, stupid. It's part of my uniform. I'm a working man, didn't you know?"

Ben chuckled and said, "I suppose that broom's one of your tools, too? You bein' a workin' man and all."

These two idiots were killing me. They just didn't understand. I had a plan. I said, "That's right Ben, it is a tool I use in my line of work." I was trying my best to make my employment seem more than it was. But the bottom line was, you couldn't polish a turd. It was what it was.

Ben had a smirk as he shot back, "Yeah, my Mom's got one too."

I reared the broom at Ben's head, but he was too quick. He and Matt moved on down the sidewalk some, so that they were out of reach of me and my broom.

Matt shouted at me, "Well, while grown-ups are working, Ben and me are goin' fishin'. We just thought you would want to know. Ha, Ha!"

I reared the broom back and was about to fling it at them when Mr. Taylor stepped out of the store and said, "Hey, what's going on here." He had taken the broom from me and was waiting for an explanation.

I lowered my head and said, "Aw, it ain't nothing Mr. Taylor. It's just Matt and Ben. There teasing me about working while they loaf off at some fishin' hole."

Mr. Taylor looked in the direction of the two boys sitting on their bikes and he said to Ben, "How ya' feeling these days Ben? Getting better?"

"Yes sir, Mr. Taylor. I'm as pert as a ruttin' buck," Ben replied.

"Well, that's good to hear." Mr. Taylor said with a smile. Then to me, "Andy, I think you've done enough around here for the day. Why don't you go ahead and join them."

I said, "That's okay Mr. Taylor. I don't mind working."

"That wasn't a question son that was an order. Now, you've worked hard around here this summer, and you deserve a little vacation. So you go and enjoy yourself."

I grinned and said, "Thanks Mr. Taylor, I do like fishin'. I just didn't want you to think I was lazy." Then as an afterthought, I nodded my head towards Matt and Ben and said, "Like them two over there."

Mr. Taylor said, "I know you're not. Just remember, you'll be working two hours a day after school, and all day on Saturdays when school starts back up. Can I count on you?"

Mr. Taylor extended his hand and as I shook it I said, "Yes sir, you can count on me."

"Good boy. Now you run along before I change my mind."

I ran to the storeroom, shed the apron and donned my John Deere Tractor hat as I pushed my bike back out to the sidewalk.

Outside, we waved at Mr. Taylor as the three of us headed towards our secret fishin' hole.

Maryanne came walking up and saw the boys riding down the street. She said to her father, "Hi Daddy. Where's Andy going?"

Mr. Taylor knew his daughter was sweet on Andy, and well she should be. He was a good boy. He said, "He's gone fishin'. I gave him the rest of the day off."

Maryanne had been looking forward to spending some time at the store with Andy, but now it looked as if she wouldn't get the chance.

Mr. Taylor saw the disappointment in her face and said, "Oh for heaven's sake Maryanne, relax. He ain't leaving the country, he's just goin' fishin'. You two will have plenty of time later on to google eye each other."

Maryanne curled her bottom lip in a pout and gave her father a sullen look.

Mr. Taylor put his arm around Maryanne's shoulder and as he led her into the store, he said, "Honey, let me tell you something about boys. Men too, for that matter. We love to fish, and the sooner you get used to that, the better it will be. Now, come on inside and I'll buy you a Yoo-hoo to ease your pain."

CHAPTER 27

Sheriff Bryson was sitting in his old leather office chair reclining backwards, feet resting on his desk. He had a cup of coffee in his hand and occasionally he'd drink from the cup, but didn't realize it. He was lost in thought and his mind was wondering.

His friend Pete dominated those thoughts. From the time they were kids until present day, the memories played through his mind like an old movie.

As he sat there, he remembered the note Pete had given him. It was still in his shirt pocket and he pulled it out, unfolded it like he'd done dozens of times over the past few weeks. He read what was written.

Charlie,
    If you're reading this, then I'm already gone. I'm with my family now. Make sure Ben gets my heart. Goodbye, old friend.

He just shook his head. Pete had paid the ultimate price to save a boy he barely knew. It takes a hell of a man to do something like that, and he doubted he'd have the courage to do it himself. Of course, Pete was in a lot of pain over the loss of his wife and kids, and most certainly that played a part in what he'd done.

Even so, knowing Pete the way he did, the Sheriff was confident Pete would still have made the sacrifice to save Ben's life. He'd seen how courageous and fearless Pete had been first hand.

Back when the train had wrecked, the Sheriff had come out of his own pocket and had Pete's wife and children buried in a cemetery out back of the Carbon Hollow Baptist Church, which is located on the outskirts of the city limits. He made sure Pete was buried next to them.

Preacher Howard had agreed not to disclose who'd footed the bill back then, and did likewise with Pete's burial.

Sheriff Bryson was sad about his friend, but was content knowing that Pete was now with his family. He looked in the direction of where Pete used to sit and beat the pants off him in checkers and said, "Goodbye, Pete. I'm gonna miss you."

He sat the coffee cup in the sink and was about to lock up the office and head home when he heard a light knock on the back door. He moved quickly to it and when he opened the door, no one was there. Then he realized, it was just his mind playing tricks on him. Or was it?

Illustration 15: The Conductor Welcomes Hobo Pete

Aboard the Ghost Train

CHAPTER 28

Pete stood on the platform and stared up at the flickering light as it grew brighter. Unlike the dreams before, this one didn't seem cold as they had. In fact, it felt almost... comfortable. Then suddenly, the train was there before him almost as if it appeared rather than arrived. Pete watched the Conductor as he stepped through the passenger car door, pulled his watch from his pocket, then said, "All aboard."

Pete just stood there on the platform, until finally the Conductor looked down at him and said, "Are you boarding, sir?" Still he couldn't move and the Conductor continued, "Mr. Hanson, we are behind schedule. Will you be boarding tonight?" The Conductor stared at Pete with those red fiery looking eyes. To his own surprise, he raised a foot to the first step of the passenger car. He reached out, gripped the handrail, and pulled himself up until his other foot rested on the step.

This pleased the Conductor to no end. He said, "Welcome aboard, Mr. Hanson. Follow me. Your family is waiting for you."

Pete followed the Conductor into the passenger car until he was standing before his wife, son, and daughter.

The Conductor leaned in and whispered into Pete's ear, "You made the right choice, Mr. Hanson. The boy was about to take your place aboard this train."

Pete was looking into the eyes and faces of his family when the Conductor said, "Please take a seat sir. We must be on our way."

Pete's wife motioned to the vacant seat next to her and he found himself sliding into it without speaking.

Neither of them spoke in fact, they just smiled at each other. He suddenly realized that he didn't hurt anymore. The pain was gone. He felt the train lurch forward.

As the train disappeared around the foggy bend, the Conductor stood at the door of the last car and shouted in a deep rumbling voice, "Alllll Abooooard!"

Illustration 16: Hobo Pete's Wife and Children

Wait for Him on the Ghost Train

EPILOGUE

That was 1963 and we never heard the Ghost Train again. Also we ain't dead either. Well, at least not yet anyway.

Maryanne and I saw each other every chance we could and I continued working in her father's store. I graduated in 1969 and the very next day I went down to the recruiting office and joined the Army. The country was at it hot and heavy in Vietnam and I felt obliged to do my part. Matt followed me there two years later and by the grace of God, we both made it home safely.

After Vietnam, Matt went to college on a VA loan and moved to Houston after graduating. He's done quite well for himself, and now he's some hotshot businessmen. He married a Mexican girl and they have two children of their own, who are both in college. They've even got a funny looking dog they named Pete.

Ben surprised us all by proposing to Andrea Fisher, Maryanne's best friend and to even bigger surprise, she accepted.

They moved across the state line into Kentucky and Ben manages a discount tire store. Andrea's a school teacher. They have six children and four grandchildren. I guess old Pete's heart is holding up pretty good.

Bo Barnett decided to dodge the draft and the last we saw of him he was boarding a Greyhound for Canada. The last we heard, he'd moved to Hollywood to try his hand at acting, but apparently failed miserably. Now he's a bartender in a Holiday Inn somewhere.

I still work at Taylor's Grocery Store, only now Maryanne and I own it. Oh, didn't I tell you? Maryanne and I got married, and had a couple of kids.

Our first child died in 91' in the first Gulf war. Joshua hadn't been there a week when the Humvee he was riding in was bombed by an I.E.D. He was just 19 years old.

Katie, our second child, is 29 years old and married to a

soldier. He's an Army Lieutenant stationed in Iraq. His name's Kevin Walsh and they have a son who's the spitting image of his father. His name's Dustin, but I like to call him "Peanut."

Of the old folks well, they're almost all gone. Doc Martin passed away in 1978 at the age of 67. Colon cancer took him quickly.

Sheriff Bryson died in an auto accident in 1981. His police cruiser rolled down an embankment after he'd lost control of it on a stormy night. His son, who was his deputy, was unanimously elected as the new Sheriff and is doing a fine job.

Mr. Taylor died of a heart attack the same year we lost Joshua in the Gulf. Mrs. Taylor is in a nursing home and suffers from Alzheimer's. She barely knows who she is, most of the time.

Dad died in 99', also from a heart attack. Mom died the following year from a broken heart.

The Gordons, Ben's parents, are still around and getting along pretty good considering their age.

Maryanne and I live in my childhood home on Maple Street. After my folks passed on, we moved in and fixed it up like new. I also restored Dad's old Chevy pickup and drive it daily.

* * * * *

I had gotten lost in the past while telling Peanut the story of Hobo Pete and the Ghost Train, and at first didn't realize he was speaking to me.

I glanced over at him and said, "I'm sorry Peanut. Did you say something?"

Peanut said, "I like that story Grandpa. I wish I could've met Hobo Pete."

"Well, I wish you could've too, Peanut. I'm sure he would've loved knowing you."

"Grandpa, can we go fishin' now?" Dustin said looking up at me with his wide blue eyes.

"Why sure we can. I just happen to know of this secret

fishin' hole where there's so many fish you might get five fish on one hook."

"Yeahhh!" Dustin shouted, then grabbed his new rod and reel and headed for the truck.

I was loading some cane poles and my tackle box into the bed of the truck when Maryanne and Katie stepped out onto the back porch. Maryanne stood there with her hands on her hips just as her Dad had done the day I first asked him for a job at his grocery store.

"And just where do you two think you're going?" Maryanne said teasingly.

"Oh honey, we was just gonna try out Peanut's new fishin' rod. We won't be long, I promise."

Katie chimed in, "I thought you were gonna help me unload the trailer," she said smiling at me.

"We won't be more than an hour, I promise."

Maryanne didn't believe me for a minute. "Mmmph, more like three hours. My Daddy warned me about you and fishin'. Well, I'll tell you two something right now, you show up after dark and you'll have to cook your own supper."

I smiled and waved as I quickly climbed into the cab of the truck. Maryanne hadn't let me cook for myself in forty years and I knew she wouldn't start now. Still, just to be on the safe side, I made a mental note to make it home before dark. No use rockin' the boat.

We were puttering along in Dad's old pickup truck and it felt like I'd gone back in time. Peanut stared out the window as I crept through town and while we were stopped at a red light on a corner of the town square, something caught Peanut's eye.

He turned to me and said excitedly as he pointed out the passenger-side window, "Grandpa! Is that Hobo Pete?"

I knew what he'd seen. In the town square was the courthouse. Situated on the front lawn of the courthouse was a statue of a soldier. At the base of the statue was a brass plate with writing on it. It read:

Captain Peter J. Hanson, U.S. Army
World War II Hero and Veteran
Carbon Hollow's Beloved Son - 1921-1963

I nodded without looking towards the statue and said, "That's him Peanut. Hobo Pete. A real hero."

The light changed and I put the truck in gear and slowly pulled away. Dustin stared out the window at the statue. Just before we were out of sight of Hobo Pete, I glanced in the rearview mirror and gave the statue one last look myself.

On the outskirts of town, I eased down on the pedal and picked up speed a little. As I did, the cane poles and bobbers were blowing in the wind as they hung out the back of the truck bed.

I smiled to myself, remembering my old friend.

The End.

Illustration 17: Andy Takes his Grandson Fishing

UP AND COMING

If you enjoyed Hobo Pete and the Ghost Train, then you won't want to miss the exciting continuing adventures of the boys from Carbon Hollow. Watch for the next installment in the series.

Book II

Hobo Pete and the Ghost Train
Joshua's Courage

Hobo Pete and 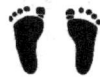 the Ghost Train
Joshua's Courage

PROLOGUE

The loud boom of a thunderclap shook me from a deep sleep. My heart was pounding and I trembled as I sat upright on the bed. I looked over and saw that Andrea was still sound asleep. We'd been married forty years and she would wake most nights at the slightest sound. Strange.

Had I only been dreaming, I thought. I climbed from the bed and looked out the window. Hmmm; not a cloud in the sky just a bright full moon.

When I glanced at the clock on the night stand it was straight up midnight. Then I heard a loud train whistle. Only it wasn't the sound of a whistle. It was the sound of people screaming, lots of people. The Ghost Train! My god it was back.

I stood in the kitchen staring at the coffee maker as the

coffee dripped into the glass pot. My mind wasn't on the coffee though. All I could think about was the ghost train.

It had been fifty years since the last time I heard it. Why Now? Why after all these years had it come back? I knew of only one reason for hearing the Ghost Train. It was searching for someone. Someone who'd died or was about to die.

Was it me the train was looking for. As far as I knew I was in good health. The heart Pete had given me was holding up well. Although between the two of us there was more than a hundred years of wear and tear on it. I was trying to sort it out when a voice from behind me said, "Boo!" I'll tell you I just about peed my pants right there on the spot. I thought I was alone and maybe I'd imagined it. After all I was a little spooked by the Ghost Train.

I was almost afraid to turn around but then I heard laughing. It was a loud raspy laugh. The laugh turned into coughing and when I got the nerve to look behind me there he stood. It was Hobo Pete.

All I could do was stand there with my mouth wide open. Pete was sitting at the kitchen table and when he finished laughing he stood and walked up to me until he was just inches from my face.

I couldn't move. But I could smell him. It was the same smell we kids had smelled the first time we'd met Pete fifty years ago.

Pete said, "What's the matter old friend, you look like you've seen a ghost." Then he broke into laughter again. He laughed and coughed and finally sat back down.

I finally got the nerve to speak. I said, A-Are y-you really h-here? Is this a d-dream?"

"I'm afraid it's not a dream Ben. Your wide awake, we're in your kitchen and yes I am a ghost. Does that clear it up for you?"

"I-It can't be. G-ghosts aren't r-real."

"Come on Ben, will you stop with the stuttering. We need to talk. I've got business to take care of and I need your help.

2

Bring your coffee over here and have a seat."

I poured a cup of coffee and about spilled it I was shaking so badly. When I offered Pete a cup he held up his hand and said, "I quit fifty years ago." I was almost embarrassed; of course he'd given it up. He was a ghost. Ghosts don't drink coffee. Or do they? Aw, how the heck would I know? I'd never met a ghost before, until now.

When I sat my coffee cup on the table and sat down Pete said, "Ben, you look great. You're a little pale, but you look great. How's the old ticker holding up?"

I couldn't believe I was sitting here talking to a fifty year old ghost. I said," It's been good to me Pete. I haven't been sick a day in my life."

Pete just sat there smiling at me. Finally I said," You know, I never got to thank you. You saved my life."

It was an awkward moment for us both. Pete had given his life, and heart, to save a young boy he barely knew. I'd thanked him a million times over the years in my prayers.

As if reading my mind Pete said," I've heard every time. I couldn't have given it to a more appreciative boy than you. Besides, you saved me too."

I was astonished. How could that be, I thought. Pete continued as if reading my thoughts, "Ben, I was miserable when I met you, Andy and Matt. In a lot of pain too. I missed my family deeply and being around you boys reminded me of what I was missing from my own children. I guess we all needed each other didn't we?"

I half smiled and said," We sure did."

"Hey by the way, how are Andy and Matt?"

"They're doing fine Pete. Matt lives in Houston Texas and he's married himself a Hispanic girl, and they have two great kids.

Andy still lives in Carbon Hollow. He and Maryanne got hitched right after he came back from Viet Nam. They own Taylor's Grocery, Maryanne's fathers' old store. Do you remember Maryanne and her father?"

Pete and I sat there like two long lost friends getting caught up on old times. And I guess that's what it was too! Only difference was, Pete was a ghost.

I was making a second pot of coffee when a thought occurred to me. I asked, "Pete, can you tell me more about the ghost train."

Pete's face grew somber looking. He said, "Aw Ben, why do you want to know about the train. There's nothing good to tell about it."

I carried another cup of coffee to the table and said, "We've always been curious about the train Pete. Where it comes from, where it goes. It's all so mysterious. But if it's too painful to talk about, then I won't press you about it."

Pete hung his head as if praying. After a moment of silence he raised his head and said, "Okay Ben, I'll tell you about the trains. You're going to need to know anyway if we plan to work together."

I said with a stutter again, "D-Did y-you say t- trains? As in m-more than o-one? And w-what k-kind of w-work are you t-talking about?"

I sat and listened without interrupting Pete as he told the secrets of the Ghost Train. It was an unbelievable story and had someone else told it to me I would have thought it just a fairy tale. But this was coming from a ghost and I hung on every word.

Pete said," The night I boarded that train was incredibly hard on me. The truth was, I'd really taken a liking to you boys and didn't want to leave you. Although leaving a part of me behind felt good and I'm happy to see its' served you well."

Pete pointed to my chest where his heart had been for fifty years. Without Pete's heart I would not have made it. He continued," Seeing my family after all those years was quite emotional. I learned that the train could not make it to its destination until I was on that train. For years it had searched for me and since I was finally on board all the passengers including my wife, children and myself could finally make it to

4

the main station where we would connect with other trains going in different directions."

"You see, Lacon Mountain in Carbon Hollow has this huge train station sitting deep below the earth's surface. It's like a Grand Central Station for ghost trains." I sat next to my wife that night and looked out the window as we drove right into the mountainside. In no time at all we pulled into Lacon Train Station. It was a strange place. There were hundreds of trains pulling into and out of the station and thousands of passengers unloading and loading. The strange part was, there was only one ticket booth." "My family and I took our place in line with all the other passengers and even though the line was enormous it went quickly. We were standing before the Ticketmaster in no time at all."

As my wife stepped to the window I looked around at all the trains coming and going. They were of all sizes and styles. Some were new and shiny and some were over a hundred years old."

I sat with my eyes wide open and a lump in my throat as I listened to Pete's story.
Pete then explained," The Ticketmaster was a thin, pale man with a sweaty white shirt with black garters on his sleeves. He was bald on top but had long scraggly hair on the sides. He wore a sun visor made of green plastic and never looked up. He just stamped your boarding pass for your final destination."

"It was then that I realized there were only two directions one could go."

I was silently praying Pete would say East or West, or even North or South. But somehow I knew it was neither.

Pete knew Ben was waiting to hear what he had to say about the directions and he said, "Up or down."

Without expecting it; I farted right there at the kitchen table.

Pete said," Come on man, haven't you grown out of that yet. Your sixty years old."

"I know but I always fart when I get scared."

5

Pete smiled briefly, remembering Ben's flatulence problem when he was a boy, but his face got a somber look again as he continued his story." The Ticketmaster stamped my wife's boarding pass without even looking at her. She showed it to me smiling; "UP" was stamped on it. The same thing happened with our children. The Ticketmaster never once looked up. That is until it came to me."

I said to Pete," Oh man, he didn't stamp yours "Down" did he? How could he after the way you've been."
Pete stared at me for the longest time, and then he said, "The Ticketmaster just smiled at me through his rotten teeth and red fiery looking eyes and said, well, looks like we got us a rail rider here haven't seen your kind around in a while."

"What's a rail rider, I asked him?" He just stamped my boarding pass real hard and lowered his head again. When I looked down at the pass the number 13 was stamped on it. No, up or down, just 13. I turned to show it to my wife and kids but they were gone. I couldn't find them anywhere." "I walked around the station aimlessly searching for my family until I found myself standing in front of the same train we'd come in on. I looked up and saw the Number 13 in big letters hanging from a post. I was at terminal 13." "A door opened on one of the passenger cars and out walked the evil conductor. He stepped down onto the platform and stood in front of me. So Mr. Hanson, it's you. I should have known. Especially after that stunt you pulled giving your heart to that boy. Now I guess I am stuck with you for a while."
"What do you mean? I asked the conductor, where is my family?"
"Your family's already gone Mr. Hanson. They caught that new shiny bullet train headed straight UP. You on the other hand have been assigned to this train."
"Assigned to this train? I don't understand."
The conductor nodded his head in the direction of terminal "1". Sitting at the terminal was a long sleek bright red bullet train. Even the smoke coming from the trains' engines was red.

Standing on the platform next to the train was this tall figure of a man with long dark hair, a chiseled face and dark deep set eyes. He wore a red cape and held a cane. Just then he turned towards us and as he smiled his eyes glowed red.

The conductor said, "That's my boss. He's not happy with me. Says I took too long to get you here and now I'm stuck with you. Up or down, which way will it be? You were headed down but then you go and save that boy. Now it seems you're stuck in the middle, and I'm stuck with you. Now we must get to work at once to see which direction you and I will both be heading."

"And what kind of work might that be?" Pete asked.

The conductor put a hand on Pete's shoulder and said, "We're going out in search of young kids who have all but given up on life or who are standing in harm's way. Our duty is to fill this train with two hundred of those young passengers."

"And what if I say no to help you and just take my Down ticket now?"

"It doesn't work that way Mr. Hanson. You see you must help me or your family will not make it to their final destination. No sir; that train will be turned around. You have only one choice. Help me fill my train, save your family and who knows maybe you'll get your own train one day. Maybe even this one."

"And you, what do you get out of the lives of two hundred kids?"

"I get that." The conductor said pointing towards the bright red bullet train.

Pete stared at the man with the red eyes standing next to the bullet train as the conductor said, "Come along now Mr. Hanson. All Abooooooaaaaaard!"

"Holy crap Pete, that's the scariest story I've ever heard. But what happened after that. You didn't help him did you? Surely not!"

Pete said, "Ben, I boarded that train but couldn't help him gather up those kids. I've figured out a way to save them but I can't do it myself. I need your help. And we have to act fast."

"Me, how am I supposed to help? There's so many. How can one man and a ghost save two hundred kids?"

"We have to Ben. We cannot fail. We will save them one at a time. Now, are you ready?"

"Where are we going? I asked not sure what I'd just agreed to.

Pete said, "Topeka, Kansas."

"What's in Topeka?" I asked.

"A boy named Joshua."

ABOUT THE AUTHOR

Sandy Pheat. Much of what we know of Sandy is from old folk lore and other talk "about town." Like the mysteries surrounding the adventures of Hobo Pete in "Hobo Pete and the Ghost Train" we have to assume that Sandy has always been there to root for the underdog, prefers good over evil, and endeavors to be a contribution verses a burden to society.

Something we can be sure of is that this Texas native author intends for the literary benefits of this book to be a gift to young people and families everywhere.

"Just as with a parent's child, a fond memory always comes with a pair of sandy feet."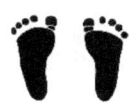